"Who are you?"

The man's familiar smile grew, warming his dark eyes and sending her heart back into a rapid frenzy.

Because his eyes looked familiar, too?

No, that couldn't be it. It had to be because he was tall, gorgeous and casually sexy in jeans and a button-down blue-striped shirt, pulled tight across nice shoulders.

Her gaze dropped to his feet.

Yep, cowboy boots, too.

Quickly blaming her renewed shortness of breath on her weakness for men in cowboy boots, Tanya looked him in the eye again, offered a raised eyebrow and waited.

"I'm a friend of the man who lives here," he finally said. "The name's Murphy. Devlin Murphy."

Devlin?

Just like that, the memory of a stolen night a decade ago in Reno came back to her. After all these years who would've thought the first person she'd run into in this town would be the same drunken fool she'd shared an almost perfect evening with.

A fool who clearly had no idea who she was.

* * *

WELCOME TO DESTINY:
Where fate leads to falling in love

Dear Reader,

Last year, I introduced you to a new family in my Welcome to Destiny series, the Murphys, six brothers who are in all stages of love from "never again" to "happy newlywed." My April 2012 release, *Having Adam's Baby,* featured the eldest brother, Adam.

Now it's Devlin Murphy's turn....

A year ago, Devlin was the fun-loving and freewheeling younger brother, but a horrific crash has him fighting old demons...physically, mentally and emotionally. He's finally back on his feet, but his choices at this point are to either accept his limitations and get on with his life or take a chance on the alternative healing methods performed by a woman who strikes a familiar chord deep inside him.

Thanks to losing her job and her boyfriend all in the same night, Tanya Reeves is ready to start her life over again. Her visit back to Destiny is just a short stay and the last thing she wants is to spend time with a man who obviously doesn't remember their one-night stand years ago. But Dev's pain calls to the healer in her. Now she has to find a way to treat the patient and hide her growing feelings for the man until she can get out of town.

Neither Dev nor Tanya were looking for love, which made writing their happily-ever-after so much fun! Please stop by my website, www.christynebutler.com, to say hello—I can also be found on Facebook and Twitter!

Happy Reading,

Christyne

Flirting with Destiny

Christyne Butler

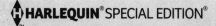
HARLEQUIN®SPECIAL EDITION®

Recycling programs
for this product may
not exist in your area.

ISBN-13: 978-0-373-65771-1

FLIRTING WITH DESTINY

Copyright © 2013 by Christyne Butilier

This edition published by arrangement with Harlequin Books S.A.

For questions and comments about the quality of this book, please contact us
at CustomerService@Harlequin.com.

® and TM are trademarks of Harlequin Enterprises Limited or its corporate
affiliates. Trademarks indicated with ® are registered in the United States Patent
and Trademark Office, the Canadian Trade Marks Office and in other countries.

Printed in U.S.A.

Books by Christyne Butler

Harlequin Special Edition

Silhouette Special Edition

Harlequin Books

Other titles by this author available in ebook format.

CHRISTYNE BUTLER

fell in love with romance novels while serving in the United States Navy and started writing her own stories six years ago. She considers selling to Harlequin Special Edition a dream come true and enjoys writing contemporary romances full of life, love, a hint of laughter and perhaps a dash of danger, too. And there has to be a happily-ever-after or she's just not satisfied.

She lives with her family in central Massachusetts and loves to hear from her readers at chris@christynebutler.com. Or visit her website, www.christynebutler.com.

To Jennifer Schober
Thank you...for everything

Chapter One

"Hey, cowboy." The blonde barmaid leaned across the three-foot expanse of aged wood. "I know just what you need to make your day complete."

Devlin Murphy glanced up from his mouthwatering burger and thick-cut fries, the house specialty here in the Blue Creek Saloon. He wasn't really a cowboy, despite the black Stetson perched on his head. She must be new and it'd been a while since he'd been in here.

Eight long months to be exact.

His brothers had tried to coax him to his old stomping grounds a few times since he'd gotten his feet back under him—literally. Devlin just hadn't been ready.

But spring had come early in Destiny, Wyoming, and on this warm, late April afternoon, Dev decided it was past time to rejoin the world of the living.

He bumped up the brim of his hat and offered what he hoped was more of his old prowler grin than his recent

pain-filled grimace. Not an easy feat thanks to the familiar white-hot fire crawling down both shoulders toward
his elbows.

"Oh, yeah? What's that?"

"Just one minute." She offered a quick wink and then
turned away.

That simple gesture did nothing for him. Not anymore.

This time last year he would've been all over that sug-
gestive sign, making sure he left with her phone number,
if not the lady herself.

Now? Not interested.

And wasn't that just another kick in the ass to go along
with the butt whipping he'd taken since the helicopter
crash that had left him and his eldest brother, Adam,
stranded for three days in the Grand Tetons National Forest.

A helicopter he'd been piloting.

Thankfully Adam had come out with just a few bruises
and scratches. Dev had been the one who'd spent five
months in the hospital dealing with a broken leg and two
broken arms. His recovery had been slow and painful, and
while he could finally take care of himself again, he'd hit
a brick wall with his physical therapy. When he bothered
to go, the weekly sessions were painful, without any last-
ing results to show for his efforts.

Of course, sitting at a bar with a straight-on view of
the rows of bottles waiting to be mixed and poured for the
saloon's patrons probably wasn't the smartest thing to be
doing right now. Not with three of his former best friends
staring back at him.

Jim Beam, Jack Daniels and Johnny Walker.

Yes, he and the boys went way back. Back to before he
could even drive. But the four of them hadn't pulled an
all-nighter in six years.

That didn't mean the desire had left him.

No, that stayed with him every day.

Just then the barmaid returned and placed a frosty mug of freshly poured beer in front of him.

Every pain-filled muscle in Devlin's body froze.

"Here you go." She offered a toothy grin. "You look like a man who's earned a tall, cold one."

Dev kept his gaze glued to the glass, the golden color calling to him like buried treasure to a weary pirate. White frothy foam lapped against the rim while beads of condensation chased one another down the length of the mug until they soaked the paper napkin below.

He swallowed, his forearms pressing hard into the rolled edge of the bar as his fingers curled into tight fists. A deep inhale through his nose caused the yeasty, bitter flavor he still remembered to come alive again inside his mouth.

Damn, coming here had been a bad idea.

"Uh." He paused and blinked hard, breaking the hypnotic hold the beer had over him. After clearing his throat, Dev looked up at the barmaid and tried to summon the courage to set her straight. "I don't—"

"Lisa, why don't you take care of the crew at the end of the bar?" A strong feminine voice cut him off. "I'll take over here."

The blonde turned and looked at her boss, Racy Steele, the fiery redhead whose personality matched her name even though she was happily married to the town's sheriff and was the mother of twins.

"But I'm talking to— I mean, I'm helping…"

Dev sat silently as the two women stared each other down. He knew who would win, and sure enough, when Racy tilted her head slightly, the barmaid shrugged and turned away.

With the ease of experience, Racy made the beer disappear, replacing it with a tall glass of ice water. "Sorry about that. She's new."

Dev nodded, releasing a deep breath.

"It's good to see you up and on your feet again," Racy continued, offering an easy smile. "You've been away from the Blue Creek for too long."

"Been away from everything too long."

"Of course, when you are here you usually don't sit at the bar."

Another defense mechanism.

When he'd decided to give up the booze, he refused to give up the friendships or the fun. Somehow sitting in one of the booths or the tables scattered around the large dance floor made the ongoing battle easier to fight.

"Yeah, I know." He grabbed a fry and popped it into his mouth.

"And you rarely come in alone."

He'd waved to a couple of familiar faces when he'd first come inside, but purposely kept walking until he reached the bar, determined to do this by himself.

"Everyone's working," he finally said. "You know, being how it's Wednesday."

Racy braced her elbows on the bar, leveling a familiar stare that told him she wasn't buying his flimsy excuse. A move she'd probably perfected over the years from dealing with Blue Creek customers. "Except you?"

"No, I'm back behind the desk at the family business."

Finally. Only whenever he sat for longer than an hour in front of the bank of computers that he used to design the home security systems sold by Murphy Mountain Log Homes, his shoulders started to pulsate, sending electric shocks into his elbows and making his fingers numb.

"Just decided to get some fresh air."

"Inside a bar? At two in the afternoon?"

"I had a craving." Damn, that didn't sound right. "For a burger."

"Do you need me to call anyone?"

Her softly spoken question caused Dev's back to stiffen, his hands falling to his lap. He rubbed at the front pocket of his jeans, searching for and finding the bronze Alcoholics Anonymous medallion he always carried with him. A reminder of what he had achieved over the last six years.

"Someone like the good sheriff of Destiny?" he asked, an edge to his words.

"If you need to talk to Gage, he'll come. As a friend." Compassion filled Racy's brown eyes. "You know that, right?"

The fight disappeared as quickly as it came.

Hell, he and Gage had a history that went back to playing football together in high school. He was also the one who took Dev to his first AA meeting. "Yeah, I know."

"Or maybe there's someone else you'd like to talk to?"

Meaning his sponsor.

Mac had been there for Dev from the very beginning. They'd met at a local meeting, bonding over a shared love of flying, and soon Dev had asked the older man to be the one person he could turn to, anytime day or night, the one person who'd understand the fight Dev faced as he struggled for sanity, for sobriety.

For his life.

Dev pulled in a deep breath, and then slowly released it. The crisis had passed. He'd faced temptation before and would again. Recognizing the want and walking away was something he'd done on a daily basis, especially over the last few months. "No, thanks. I'm good."

There was that head tilt again.

"I mean it, Racy. Just let me enjoy my meal." He

paused, searching for a way to lighten the mood. His gaze flicked to the end of the bar. "And the view."

Racy grinned. "Forget it, Murphy. She's only twenty-three."

"Ouch. Now, you're making me feel old."

"You're not old." Racy fiddled with something behind the bar out of his sight. "She's just too young."

Dev reached for his burger. "Doesn't look that way from here."

"She was still in elementary school when you were going to fraternity parties at the University of Wyoming."

"Thanks a lot." Okay, that was too young even if he had been interested. Dev took a bite of his burger, chewed and then swallowed, watching as Racy hovered nearby. "You don't have to babysit me."

"I'm not babysitting." She wiped down the already clean areas on either side of him. "I'm working."

"Yeah, right."

"You do realize the Blue Creek belongs to me, right? That means I get to decide where and when—"

A buzzing noise had Racy dropping the rag and reaching for the cell phone tucked into a rear pocket. Her face lit up with a big smile as she hit a button and pressed the phone to her ear.

"Hey, honey. How's the world's sexiest sheriff?" She offered Dev a quick wink, then laughed. "Yes, I can feel you blushing from here."

Devlin just shook his head as Racy stepped away to have a private conversation with her husband. Sometimes it still amazed him that Racy and Gage, two people as different as night and day, had fallen in love and married, but he'd stood up for them at their wedding.

Something he hadn't been able to do for Adam and Fay. His sister-in-law had been almost four months pregnant by the time she and Adam had worked out their is-sues last summer, and they hadn't wanted to wait any longer to get married.

He'd ended up watching a video of their September wedding from his hospital bed, unable to keep his prom-ise to be his eldest brother's best man.

At least he'd been back on his feet, sort of, when the newest member of the Murphy family, Adam Alistair Murphy Jr., A.J. for short, had arrived back in February.

"How about a fresh piece of apple pie topped with a scoop of vanilla ice cream for dessert?"

Racy's question pulled Dev from his thoughts, and he realized she'd finished her call and had cleared away his empty plate. "No, thanks."

He climbed off the bar stool, leaning heavily against the bar as he dug for his wallet. Damn, his leg felt like jelly and he'd left the cane his physical therapist insisted he still needed in his Jeep.

"Time for me to head back to work."

She smiled and gave his hand a quick squeeze after taking his money. "You plan to stop by the firehouse on your way?"

That question caught him by surprise. "No. Why?"

"No reason. It's just that your name comes up whenever any of the team is here. I thought they'd like to know one of their best and brightest volunteers is up and around."

Yeah, up and around, but nowhere close to being able to rejoin the department. If ever. No, he wasn't ready to face his former coworkers yet.

Dev shoved his wallet back in his pocket and offered a quick prayer he wouldn't fall on his face when he turned around. "See you later, Racy. Thanks for the great meal."

"Say hi to your family."

Dev acknowledged her words with a wave, hating the

ever-present limp that marked his walk as he headed out. His family said the slight hitch in his step wasn't as noticeable as Dev thought, but it was just another reminder of how much his life had changed in the last year.

Making his way across the gravel parking lot, he opened the door to his Jeep and climbed inside, trying to ignore the fresh round of pain racing through his veins.

Maybe this hadn't been such a great idea.

As wonderful as his family had been since the accident, Dev had been desperate to get out on his own again. Lord knew he hadn't had a moment to himself in the last four months except when he was in bed at night. Even then, either one of his parents or Liam—the only brother who still lived in the log mansion that was the family home—would check in.

He appreciated all they'd done for him. Hell, with two broken arms he'd been like a baby, relying on his family for everything from his meals to bathing. It'd been three months since the casts were removed and still everyone hovered.

He needed space to think, to breathe.

And despite his father's offer to replace the four-wheel drive Wrangler with something that made it easier to get behind the wheel, Dev had insisted on keeping it—it was the vehicle he'd bought the day he kicked his drinking habit.

"But why the Blue Creek?" he asked his reflection in the rearview mirror as he turned over the engine and backed out of the parking space. "Why not go to Sherry's Diner? Or grab a sandwich at Doucette's Bakery?"

He didn't have an answer, or didn't want to come up with one, so he cranked up the radio as he slowed to a stop at the parking lot exit, waiting for the chance to pull onto the street.

Diagonally across from him was White's Liquors, a red brick building with a faded red, white and blue advertisement from the 1940s to buy war bonds still visible on the side.

When old man White had been alive, he'd had the ad repainted every five years in honor of the two brothers he'd lost during the war, but his kids owned the place now and the anniversary of the repainting had come and gone last fall without being touched up.

The traffic had cleared, but Dev still sat there, staring at the building, wondering about the ad and realizing he hadn't stepped foot inside the building in the last six years.

Hadn't needed to. Hadn't wanted to.

Until this very moment.

His grip was so tight on the steering wheel that his knuckles turned white. Pulling in a deep breath, he let go and put the Jeep in gear. Once he was on the street, he grabbed his cell phone and hit the button that connected him directly to Mac. Three rings later a buzzing noise filled his ear as Mac answered.

"Dev?"

Mac's voice came through, but the reception was terrible. Dev released the pent-up breath with one whoosh. "Yeah, it's me. Can you talk?"

"At...airport."

Dev's heart lurched. That was the last place he wanted to go. Okay, the second to last place.

"Heading...home...meet you there."

Every other word of Mac's was indecipherable, but Dev breathed a sigh of relief. "On my way."

"Dev...need to...arrived yesterday."

Circling the town square, Dev headed toward the sheriff's office and the fire station. His gaze firmly on the road ahead, he didn't allow even his peripheral vision to stray toward the open bays where a few of the firefighters were washing down the engine and the light-duty rescue truck.

"Mac, you're breaking up. This connection sucks." The tightness in Dev's chest eased as he headed out of town. "You can tell me when you see me. I'll be waiting on the front porch."

Moments later, Dev drove past the entrance to his family's ranch and the turnoff to his brother Adam's place, and kept going until he saw the road to Mac's farm. The land had been in his friend's family for generations, much like the land the Murphy M7 Ranch sat on, but it hadn't been a working farm for years.

Turning into the driveway, he started to slow to a stop near the two-story farmhouse, but noticed a car parked down near the metal hangar out back. When a storm had destroyed the unused barn almost a dozen years ago, Mac had it torn down and erected a steel structure that housed his baby, a 1929 Travel Air 4000 biplane.

Dev drove to the hangar, parking next to the plain brown sedan that sported Colorado plates. He frowned.

He and Mac had talked last week and his friend hadn't mentioned having any visitors. Maybe he planned to finally retire that hunk of junk pickup he drove and had picked up a newer used car.

Then Dev noticed the single door to the hangar looked slightly ajar. He dropped his hat in the passenger seat, climbed out of his Jeep and walked as quickly as the ache in his leg would allow to check it out.

Yep, definitely open.

Slipping inside, Dev paused a moment to let his eyes adjust to the dim interior. He skirted the protruding wing of the vintage plane Mac had lovingly restored piece by piece. His hand gently glided over the smooth fuselage even as his stomach tightened into familiar knots.

Mac had allowed Dev to help with the restoration after he'd become his sponsor, and had taken him for his first flight the day Dev had celebrated twelve months of sobriety. He'd also been the one who got Dev interested in flying helicopters and was there the day he'd earned his pilot's license.

Not that Dev ever planned to be in the air again.

Refusing to allow his thoughts to head in that direction, he kept walking, ignoring the pain, until he could've sworn he heard—

Wind chimes?

Yes, that's exactly what it sounded like, along with music that should only be heard in an elevator.

Wondering if Mac had left the radio on—though his buddy was more a fan of classic rock and roll than this stuff—Dev stepped into the back area of the hangar where Mac kept an office on one side and an all-in-one exercise machine on the other.

The sight of a very shapely feminine backside perched in the air stopped him in his tracks.

Hel-lo!

Dev took in the position of the arms and legs that went with the sexy backside. The woman was twisted tighter than a pretzel. Then she slowly untangled herself to stand straight and tall. Still facing away from him, she showed off miles of toned muscles thanks to a skimpy tank top and leggings that hugged her curves in all the right places.

And was that a tattoo on her shoulder?

Not wanting to startle whoever she was, Dev cleared his throat. Nothing. Was the music too loud for her to hear him?

He tried again but all she did was gracefully move into another position that left her balancing on one leg, arms stretched high over her head. She tilted her head back, a ponytail of dark hair brushing between her shoulder blades.

Impressive. If he tried that, even when he'd had two good legs, he'd be flat on his butt in two seconds.

Figuring the intruder was harmless, Dev took a few more steps and then leaned back against Mac's desk. Crossing his arms over his chest, he ignored the pain the move brought and decided to enjoy the show.

He let his gaze travel the length of her, surprised when he felt his body responding in a way it hadn't in months.

Not that he'd spent much time with the opposite sex since the crash, but this stranger was intriguing him in ways the blonde barmaid hadn't even come close to.

Who was she?

Mac had a daughter from a long-ago marriage. Still, this woman was too young. Dev guessed she was in her late twenties, a few years younger than him.

She couldn't be a girlfriend, could she? The last he knew, the feisty Ursula, owner of the local beauty parlor his mother visited every week, was the current object of Mac's affections.

Maybe she was another lost soul looking for redemption?

His buddy had helped many members of the local Alcoholics Anonymous chapter over the years, often letting those who needed a place to crash stay in the otherwise empty cabin.

But Mac always kept his assistance to the male species. It was just simpler that way.

Surprised that the idea of her possibly being off-limits bothered him, Dev tucked away his growing interest. Time to make his presence known once and for all.

Looking away from her bare feet, he cleared his throat

one more time and said, "Miss, I don't mean to scare you—"

She whirled around, and suddenly a barrage of foam bricks flew at him, pelting him on his shoulders, the last one bouncing off his chin, cutting off his words.

More surprised than hurt, he easily deflected the next two bricks aimed at his head. Jerking away from the desk, he cursed under his breath as the familiar fire ripped down his leg and he wobbled like a newborn.

"Hey! Knock it off!"

Tanya Reeves stood, arm cocked, her breaths coming hard and fast, ready to hurl her last yoga brick at the tall stranger's head. Her heart pounded in her chest, the hard-earned peace and tranquility from her yoga session blown to bits the moment she'd turned and found him behind her.

"Who are you?" she demanded, between huffs. "What are you doing here? Don't you dare come one step closer."

"I haven't taken a step yet."

She dropped the brick and grabbed her cell phone from the cushioned bench attached to the nearby weight machine. "You better not. I'm dialing 9-1-1 right now."

"It's not going to do you any good."

She scooted back a foot and took a stance, pushing her sweaty bangs out of her eyes. It'd been a few years since her last karate class, but she could still deliver a round-house kick with the best of them.

Of course, this guy had to be almost six feet tall. *Better shoot for the chest.* "Yeah, well, we'll see about that."

The man perched himself against the desk again, his arms at his sides, fingers curling around the scarred edge. The corner of his mouth quirked into a slight grin.

A familiar grin?

"There's no reception in here," he continued.

She looked down at her phone. No bars. Damn!

"Don't worry. You're safe with me."

Yeah, if I had a dollar for every time I'd heard that. A snort of disbelief escaped before she could stop it.

"I take it from your response you don't believe me."

Tanya relaxed, but kept a safe distance away. She was probably overreacting, but life had a way of teaching hard lessons. "I might if I knew your name and what you're doing here."

His smile grew, easy and natural, warming his icy blue eyes and sending her heart back into a rapid frenzy.

Because his eyes looked familiar, too?

No, that couldn't be it. It had to be because he was tall, gorgeous and casually sexy in jeans and a button-down blue-striped shirt, pulled tight across nice shoulders.

Her gaze dropped to his feet.

Yep, cowboy boots, too.

Quickly blaming her renewed shortness of breath on her weakness for men in cowboy boots, Tanya looked him in the eye again, offered a raised eyebrow and waited.

"I'm a friend of the man who lives here," he finally said. "The name's Murphy. Devlin Murphy."

Devlin?

And just like that, the memory of a stolen night a decade ago in Reno came back to her. After all these years, who would've thought the first person she'd run into in this town was the same drunken fool she'd shared what had been an almost-perfect evening with?

A fool who clearly had no idea who she was.

Chapter Two

"Your turn."

Tanya blinked, chasing away memories of bright lights, crowded casinos and dark nightclubs where the same strong arms of the man in front of her had once held her close. "Huh?"

"It's only fair that you tell me your name now."

She wondered for a moment if he'd remember her. Until Devlin had said his name, she hadn't realized who he was, but she blamed that on turning in the middle of a side stretch and finding a total stranger watching her.

No, not a total stranger.

Yes, actually he was.

Ten years was a long time, and just because they'd spent one night together didn't mean they knew each other.

Of course, she'd known in a town the size of Destiny chances were good she'd run into him during her stay. Who would've thought it'd happen on her first day back?

"Tanya," she finally answered him, lowering her voice when the music shut off. "Tanya Reeves."

She watched his eyes. His face. Not a hint of recognition flickered there. Okay, that stung, but she shouldn't be surprised. He'd been partying pretty heavily the night they'd met. A party that had continued until the wee hours of the next morning before they'd ended up back in his fancy hotel room….

"Pleased to meet you, Tanya." His words cut into her thoughts. "Now, can I ask how you got in here?"

She dropped her hands to her hips, the need to call for help forgotten. "How I— How did *you* get in here?"

"I have a key. One I didn't have to use because the door was open."

No, that wasn't right. She'd made sure she closed it behind her.

"You have to jiggle the handle to make sure the latch catches," he continued, as if he'd read her mind. "Otherwise, you never know who might walk in."

Tanya crossed her arms, suddenly conscious of her lack of clothing. Why it bothered her now when she practically lived in yoga wear she didn't want to think about.

Heck, the night she'd met Devlin Murphy she hadn't been wearing much more than feathers and sequins. A lot of sequins.

"Thanks for the tip. I'll keep it in mind for the future."

"So, you plan to do…" His voice trailed off as he waved a hand in the air. "Whatever that was you were doing again?"

"Daily."

His mouth pressed into a hard line and he gripped the edge of the desk. Did the idea of her working out here bother him that much? Why should he care?

"And what I was doing is called yoga. Anusara yoga,

to be exact," she added. "It's not as demanding as other forms, but after sleeping last night on that lumpy mattress in the cabin— Hey, are you okay?"

He released his tight hold on the desk, but Tanya saw the fine sheen of sweat on his forehead.

"Yes, I'm fine."

She'd heard about the horrific accident he'd been in last summer—it had even made the papers in Denver, the well-known names of the victims jarring her memory. Once he and his brother had been found safe, the story had disappeared from the news, but the last reports had said that Devlin would be hospitalized for months.

"I asked because you look like you're in pain."

His jaw tightened further. "I'm not. Did you just say you slept in the cabin?"

Tanya nodded, not believing his denial for a moment. "Mac offered me one of the spare bedrooms in the farmhouse, but I'm used to having my own space. He also told me the second key on the key ring was to this place and I was free to—"

"Wait a minute, you have—" Surprise registered over his handsome features. "Why would Mac give you a key to the hangar?"

"Why would he give you one?" she shot back.

"Because we're friends."

"Well, we're family."

Devlin's mouth literally dropped open. "You're what?"

"Steve Mackenzie is my grandfather." The shock on his face had Tanya wondering if Devlin and Mac were as good friends as he claimed. "Didn't you know he had a family?"

"A daughter, yes, but they haven't been in touch— I mean, they were— They'd just started to…"

"Work things out?" she offered when he stumbled over his words. "That's true. There were a lot of years he and my mother didn't talk, didn't have anything to do with each other actually, but that changed last fall. Mac came to visit just after Thanksgiving, and of course, my mom wanted me there, too. She thought it was time we got to know each other again."

"Again?"

This time, Tanya smiled and took pity on him. "My mom and I lived here in Destiny with Mac until my eighth birthday."

"Really?"

"Really."

A fact she'd never shared with him that night ten years ago after he'd told her who he was and where he was from. Not that it would've helped her earn a spot in his memory.

"Yeah, I remember Mac mentioning his daughter living with him for a couple of years, but that's all." He pulled in a deep breath and slowly released it, the tension leaving his jaw as that same charming smile she remembered came to his lips. "So you're here for a visit."

Her heart started that crazy pounding again.

Setting down her cell phone and grabbing her towel, Tanya held the cotton material to her chest, thankful for the way it draped down the center of her body as she patted at the sweat drying on her skin. "Actually, I came to help Mac."

"Help, how?"

"I'm assuming you know about the arthritis in his hands?" Devlin nodded, but remained silent so she continued. "Well, I'm a licensed acupuncturist. We did a few sessions during his time in Denver, and it seemed to help with his pain. When the chance came for me to come here and work with him again, I agreed."

"Did you say acupuncture?" Devlin asked, swearing under his breath. "As in needles?"

"Yes, that's what she said."

Tanya turned at the low, gravelly voice of her grandfather.

"Hey, Mac," she said, using his nickname. Calling him Granddad didn't feel right, given the fragile state of their renewed relationship.

As she looked at him, she was still amazed at how much the man looked like Jimmy Buffett. She'd told him so when they'd reconnected back in November, surprised to find out her grandfather was as much of a fan of the famed musician as she was. "When did you get here?"

"A few minutes ago and just in time, it seems." He joined them, stopping to stand between her and Devlin and glancing at the brick-strewn floor of the hangar. "Good to see you, Dev. I tried to tell you about Tanya's visit, but my phone kept cutting out on me."

Mac dropped a battered backpack at his feet. He held out his hands, clenching and releasing his fingers. "This damn knuckle-busting arthritis is tough on the flying. I'm sure glad she's here."

"Yeah, so I heard," Dev finally said. "But needles? Really?"

Mac laughed and pushed the brim of his ball cap higher on his forehead. "Yeah, no big surprise I didn't tell you about that, either. Besides, I didn't just want Tanya here to help with my aching bones. We've been in touch quite a bit thanks to emails and phone calls the last few months, but we've still got a lot of catching up to do."

"After twenty years apart, I'd say so."

"Twenty-three."

Mac's reply overlapped Tanya's and she laughed, returning Mac's grin.

"Am I missing the joke?" Devlin asked.

"My mom and Mac had their first disagreement during their reunion over exactly how long it'd been since they'd seen each other," Tanya explained. "Once they finally agreed on the number of years, it sort of became a running joke."

"At the least, it's a tension breaker. Which is a good thing, because I guess I can now admit to having ulterior motives for getting Tanya back to Destiny again," Mac said.

Tanya saw the craftiness in the old man's dark brown eyes as he glanced at Devlin. Figuring out what he meant took a matter of seconds. "Oh, no. No way."

"Tanya, you're exactly what he needs."

She shook her head, knowing her instincts about the pain Dev had been trying to hide were right on target. But her own instincts about needing to stay far away from trouble—work trouble and man trouble in particular— were also on the mark.

Devlin Murphy was trouble with a capital *T*. "Not interested, Mac."

"You worked wonders for me, in ways that regular medication hasn't for years. I just want you to do the same for my friend."

"Friend?" Dev finally spoke up. "Wait a minute, you mean me?"

Tanya ignored him and turned to face her grandfather, still shocked by his suggestion. "You know I have plans to be in London for my advanced studies class in a couple of months. I don't have time to do a full workup based on whatever Devlin's current physical therapy status might be."

"I'm only suggesting you supplement the therapy Dev is already doing," Mac pushed. "Lord knows, the man needs all the help he can get."

Maybe so, but not from me.

"Yes, from you," Mac continued as if he could read her mind. "No one else in this town does what you do."

"So he can go to Laramie or Cheyenne." Tanya spun away, looping the towel over her neck. Grabbing her mat, she quickly rolled it and shoved it into her bag. "There must be someone in either of those places who specializes in my field."

"Yeah, right." Mac jerked a thumb in Dev's direction. "The guy blows off more PT sessions than he makes. There's no way he'd go for any other type of treatment."

"So why would you think he'd work with me?"

"Hey, can I get a word in here?" Devlin asked.

"No!"

Again with the simultaneous answer. Tanya shot Mac a dark look and headed across the room to retrieve the yoga bricks she'd thrown at Devlin.

Of all the nerve!

Here she thought she and Mac had become closer over the last couple of months. Growing up with her mother's stories of her grandfather's alcoholic outbursts contradicted the memories she'd had of a sweet man who baked cookies, watched old television shows with her and took her for long walks around the farm.

She'd hoped by coming back to Destiny she could recapture the special bond they'd had when she'd been a child. Instead, he wanted her to provide free care to his friends!

Finding out she'd been accepted into the prestigious International Academy of Traditional Chinese Medicine in the United Kingdom had been a godsend after leaving the clinic where she'd worked for the last four years. Being told she either had to resign or she would be fired from a job she loved had been a very dark time in her life.

She'd lost more than employment that day, and she was finally seeing the light at the end of a long, gloomy tunnel.

When Mac had suggested she spend her last two months in the States with him, she'd been overjoyed. Not that she didn't love her mom, stepfather and stepsisters, but she'd always felt that she and Mac shared something special and it meant so much that he wanted her in Destiny.

Now she knew why.

Gathering her yoga bricks, she turned and came face to face with the one man in this town she never planned to get her hands on again.

"What exactly is it that you do?" Devlin's softly spoken question and the sincerity in his gaze doused her indignation, compelling her to answer him.

"Like I already told you, I'm a licensed acupuncturist." Tanya rattled off her credentials, knowing them by heart, having been asked that question many times before. "I'm also board-certified as a massage therapist—although lately I've been working mostly in aquatic therapy—and I'm a Chinese herbalist."

"Wow. That's pretty impressive."

"Thanks. Mac obviously thinks so." Filling her bag, she ducked around both men and headed for the hangar's exit, having no idea what she was going to do now. Other than drown her sorrows in a hot shower and a tall glass of wine.

On second thought, scratch the wine. She'd settle for ice-cold lemonade instead.

"Tanya, wait. Please, let me finish," Mac called out. "I'm sorry I blurted my idea out like that. Being tactful has never been my strong suit."

Not knowing why, Tanya stopped along the side of the antique plane and turned to look at him. "Yeah, I'm learning that about you."

"I swear I didn't bring you here under false pretenses. Remember how we'd talked about you helping me during your stay to bump up your savings for your living expenses overseas?"

Tanya nodded and bit hard at her bottom lip. Damn, he got her right where it hurt the most. Her wallet. She'd finally paid off the last of her student loans a year ago, but losing her job had hurt her savings in more ways than she'd ever planned.

A satisfying kind of hurt, but painful nonetheless.

Even giving up her apartment and storing her stuff at her mom's place meant things were going to be tight for the next six months.

"When I got the idea of you helping Dev, which honestly only came to me a few nights ago," Mac went on, taking a few steps toward her, "I fully intended to pay for any work you do with him, in addition to my own treatments."

Well, he had her there. The extra money would mean she could experience life outside of her schooling during her time in Europe. There were so many amazing places she'd only read about or researched online that she wanted to visit.

"Like hell you will." Dev joined them, the hitch in his step visible to her trained eye. "I pay my own way."

"This was my idea," Mac protested. "I'll pay."

"Forget it, old man. If I end up going for any of that stuff, I'll cough up the cash. Besides, she doesn't sound too thrilled about taking on an extra patient."

"What stuff?" Tanya challenged. Not that she had agreed to take him on. Yet. However, helping nonbelievers understand the benefits of her work was her favorite part of the job. "You practically keeled over when I said the word acupuncture."

"Yeah, well, needles aren't my thing." He squared his shoulders, placing his weight mainly on his left leg. "And you can forget about any herbs, Chinese or otherwise."

Oh, yes, this man was hurting all over. He was doing his best to hide that fact and he probably succeeded with those with an untrained eye, but she could almost feel the pain radiating from him.

The need to ease that hurt quickly outweighed any of the reasons why she should or shouldn't do this. "You're not leaving me with much to work with."

"Oh, I don't know," Dev said, his voice suddenly shifting into a more relaxed tone. Then came that familiar grin. "A massage is always welcomed."

Hmm. The desire to show off her roundhouse kick came back to her from earlier. "Yeah, like that's the first time I've ever heard that."

Thankful for the shadows that hid the heated flush on her cheeks, Tanya cursed herself for blushing. She never had in the past when other men had been foolish enough to say the same thing to her.

She'd easily put professional athletes and ski-bum millionaires in their place when they'd tried to flirt their way through her sessions. Getting involved with a patient was a major no-no.

Not that Devlin would technically be her patient. Even if she did agree to this crazy idea…

She returned his stare, fighting the memories from the night they'd shared, a night that felt like it had happened a lifetime ago.

Because it had.

She had no idea how much Devlin had changed over the years. He could be married with three kids by now. But she was also far removed from the girl she'd been back then, too.

Could she do it?

Could she possibly work with—?

Mac loudly cleared his throat, forcing her attention

back to her grandfather. "Of course, I don't want you to do anything that would make you uncomfortable," he said. "Maybe we should just forget the whole thing. I can double my payments for the work you do with me."

"Clients are often the ones who are uncomfortable, at least until they understand what I'm accomplishing and they see the benefits of the treatments." Tanya kept her tone cool and professional as her gaze slid between the two men. "I think Devlin should observe an acupuncture session before either of us makes up our minds."

"Sure, but I won't change my mind on that." Dev rocked back on his heels for a moment, then caught himself. "But you can have Mac give me a call when you get it scheduled."

"Oh, there's no need for that. I have the cabin all set up. We're ready to go."

The smile slipped from his face. "You mean, like now?"

"That's why I was doing my yoga workout here. I don't know if you're aware of how small the cabin is and I wanted Mac to be able to have his first session in a calm place."

"Right." Dev swallowed hard. "Calm."

"So why don't I head there and take a much-needed shower?" Tanya smiled at the both of them as she backed away. "I'm sure you two can find something to talk about for the next half hour."

Mac, who stood as tall as Devlin, eyed his friend. "Yeah, I'm sure we can."

"Oh, and, Mac, you should get yourself a light meal and slip into something looser, like sweats. It's been a while since you've done this and remember what happened that first time."

He nodded. "I remember."

Dev's eyes grew wide. "What happened?"

"I tossed my cookies." Mac barked out a gruff laugh. "And that was after I fell flat on my face while getting off the damn table."

"And you *want* to do this again?" Dev's tone was incredulous.

Tanya's laughter joined her grandfather's as she reached the door. "That's what I said, too, but he was brave enough to agree to a second session just a few days later. He came through that one with flying colors."

Dev looked from Mac to her, crossing his arms over his chest again. She couldn't see his eyes from this far away, but she could guess at the emotion in their icy blue depths.

"Brave or just crazy?"

"Well, some say there's a fine line between the two," she replied. "I guess it depends which side you're standing on."

Chapter Three

"I can't believe you never told me about your grand-daughter." Dev stood next to Mac, waiting while his friend locked up the hangar.

"I can't believe how hard it is for you to keep your eyes off my granddaughter's ass."

Having no idea how to respond to that, Dev kept his mouth shut. He glanced across the yard toward the cabin, glad that Tanya had already disappeared inside and hadn't heard Mac's comment.

Silently, he admitted his disappointment that he hadn't been able to watch her walk away, because she did have a damn fine backside.

Mac headed for the farmhouse and Dev fell into step next to him, noticing how the man slowed his pace to match his own awkward stride. The thought of stopping by the Jeep for his cane crossed his mind, but Dev decided he could make the short distance across the yard without it.

Besides, if he got it now he'd have no reason not to take it over to the cottage. The last thing he wanted was for Tanya to see him hobbling around like an old man.

"Still not using the cane, huh?"

"I use it." A zing of fire licked across Dev's right hip and down his thigh. "Sometimes."

Mac just shook his head and went inside, leaving the door open for Dev to follow. His friend headed upstairs and Dev went into the kitchen, choosing to lean against the counter instead of taking a seat at the table.

If he sat down, he probably wouldn't be able to stand again.

Still, it felt good to take the weight off his legs, even just a little bit. Not that having Tanya see him with a cane mattered. She'd obviously figured out he was injured. The gleam in her intelligent brown eyes and her direct questions had told him that long before Mac had come out with his crazy idea of her helping him.

Needles? No way in hell.

There'd also been something else in the way she'd looked at him, something that didn't have anything to do with their being a potential client and caregiver and everything to do with being a man and a woman.

It hadn't lasted long. She'd managed to erase the gleam seconds after the interest lit up her eyes, but for the briefest of moments…

He glanced out the large window over the sink, his eyes following the direct sightline to the cabin. It wasn't hard to imagine Tanya's toned muscles slick with soap as she stood beneath the hot spray of the cabin's shower—

"What are you grinning at?" Mac walked into the kitchen, having switched out his jeans for sweatpants, but still wearing the same T-shirt that boasted he was a founding member of the Mile-High Club—Huey Style in faded lettering across an image of a helicopter. "Or do I want to know?"

He probably didn't, so Dev settled for a noncommittal shrug instead.

Opening the refrigerator, Mac grabbed a package of sandwich meat, cheese, mustard and a couple of water bottles. He shut the door with one hip, tossed a bottle at Dev and sat at the table. "Pass me that loaf of bread behind you."

Dev did as requested.

Mac pulled out two slices and squirted a healthy amount of the yellow condiment on both. "You want one of these?"

"No, thanks. I grabbed a burger at the Blue Creek a little while ago."

Mac stopped spreading the mustard and looked at him. "You went to the Creek for lunch?"

"Yeah." His mouth suddenly dry, Dev cranked open the water bottle and took a sip. "So?"

"Your first time back in town in months and you go to a bar?" Mac's surprised tone turned flat. "Alone?"

Dev returned his friend's stare. "Yes, alone. I did fine."

This time Mac only offered a raised eyebrow and went back to sandwich making.

"I did," Dev pushed, wondering why he felt the need to defend himself. No, that wasn't true. He knew why. He and Mac had had too many conversations like this in the past. Conversations where Mac had seen him in much worse condition than he was now. "I'm not saying it was easy. Hell, it was way harder than I'd thought it'd be. Racy stepped in, but I was...tempted."

Silence filled the air for a long moment as Mac sliced his sandwich from corner to corner into two perfect triangles. "Well, we all get tempted," he finally said.

Dev thought back to the sight and smell of that tall frosty beer. Swiping his tongue across his lips, he swore he could almost taste the forbidden liquid there. "But I got through it. I ate my burger and fries, washing it down with bland, boring ice water." He took another sip of the same. "Then I got out of there."

"Is that why you called me?"

There was no reason to lie. "Actually it was the idea of paying a visit to White's Liquors across the street after I left the bar that made me call."

Mac took a bite of his sandwich, chewed and swallowed before he spoke. "Yeah, I used to avoid that side of town like the plague. Still do at times. If you were interested in eating out, you should've come to the coffee shop at the airstrip. Everyone's been asking about you."

Dev's fingers tightened, the plastic bottle crinkling in his grip. "I already told you I have no plans to get back in the air again."

"I know you did, but that was when you were still in the hospital. I figured once you got some distance from the accident, you might've changed your mind."

"I haven't."

"I read the report. It wasn't your fault."

Mechanical failure due to electrical wiring defect. Yeah, Dev had read the report, too. Actually, he'd listened as Adam sat beside his hospital bed and read it to him a few months after the accident.

Final determination: pilot not at fault. Commended for landing disabled aircraft resulting in no loss of life. License to fly fully reinstated.

No, thanks.

Dev took another long swallow of water. "Like I said, I'm done flying."

Mac opened his own water bottle and did the same.

"Well, I guess it's a good thing Liam and Bryant started lessons last month. From what I've heard they're both doing pretty well. Should be certified in the next few weeks."

A buzzing filled his ears. Swallowing hard only expanded the noise until his head throbbed. "My broth— my brothers are taking flying lessons?"

"You didn't know?" Mac looked at him, the last bite of his sandwich frozen halfway to his mouth. "Forget I asked." He dropped his hand to the table, regret in his voice. "I can tell from your face. Sorry, man. I thought they told you."

"Flying helos?" The question sounded stupid, but he blamed it on the still faint ringing. "They're learning to fly helicopters?"

Mac nodded. "When they and your father came by looking for information on replacing the bird, I figured Liam and Bryant were backups for you. Isn't that what you always planned once it was decided having the helo was helping the family business?"

Yeah, the few months they'd had the helicopter before the crash had proved the benefit of seeing their various work sites from the air. Not to mention the ease and speed in getting to jobs located outside of Destiny.

Dev searched his brain, trying to remember if anyone in his family had talked about buying a new helicopter, much less flying the damn thing.

Faint memories of his parents weighing the needs of the business vs. the safety of their sons while sitting at his hospital bedside came back to him, but once he'd made it clear to everyone he had no intention of getting behind the controls again, he'd thought the subject was dropped.

Apparently not.

"You okay?"

Dev blinked, realizing he'd been staring at the empty water bottle held tight in his hand. As he eased his grip, the plastic crinkled and popped back into place. "Yeah, I'm okay."

Mac only nodded as he rose and cleaned up his mess. He downed the rest of his water bottle then grabbed two more from the refrigerator, tossing one at Dev. "Not to change the subject, but are you sure you want to sit in on this pincushion session?"

No, he wasn't, but it was better than heading home and dealing with his brothers and the secret they'd kept from him for the past month. "Sure. Why not? Just don't expect me to change my mind."

"About working with Tanya?"

Just the sound of her name lightened Dev's mood. "Not necessarily."

Mac shot him a dark look as they headed out the back door and across the yard, following a well-worn path to the cabin. "Why? You've already said you're not interested in any of her methods."

No, he wasn't, at least not anything that had to do with needles or munching on foreign plants. He didn't have any idea what that left in her bag of tricks, other than a massage, of course, but there'd been something about the tone of her voice when she'd spoken of her work.

She believed in what she did.

He used to feel that way about flying. About being a part of the Destiny Fire Department's volunteer squad. Two pieces of his life that were gone now. The burning aches across his shoulders, hips and down one leg were constant reminders of that fact.

And he had no one to blame but himself, no matter what that damn report said.

Dev could see his friend was waiting for an answer,

but they'd arrived at the cabin so he only said, "Let's just say she intrigues me."

"Look, seeing how Tanya and I have just started to rebuild our relationship, I don't have any right to say this…" Mac paused, one foot on the low porch that ran the length of the cabin. He glanced at the closed front door for a moment, then turned to him. "But I'm going to anyway."

Dev waited, not sure how he'd respond if Mac came right out and asked him to not to spend time with Tanya in any way, shape or form.

Up until this moment, he would've done anything his friend asked of him. Except fly.

And now, stay away from Tanya.

He had no idea why someone he'd just met fascinated him so much, but she was the first woman in the past year to make him feel like his old self, and he couldn't walk away from that.

"Telling you to stay away from my granddaughter would be like telling kids to keep out of the penny candy aisle at Packard's Store," Mac continued, his voice low. "But she's had a rough time of it for the past few months. I don't know the details, but she's been pretty down since the holidays. Until she found out about being accepted for this advanced schooling thing."

"What does that have to do with me?"

"I don't want anything—or anyone—to get in the way of her going to London."

"Hey, all I said was I'm intrigued. You know, in learning more about her work. Spending time with an interesting lady. That's it."

"Don't break her heart."

Tanya's heart was the least of her body parts that interested him. Not that he didn't care about a lady's feelings. He'd always made it clear to anyone he got involved with

that he was a here-and-now kind of guy, and not someone to get serious with. "Me? I'm a confirmed bachelor.
You know that."

Mac sighed. "As long as you remember that, and the
fact I'll break you in two if you hurt her, we're good."

A confirmed bachelor?

Well, at least that answered the wife and kids question
that had been running through her head the entire time
she'd showered and changed.

She'd reached the front door in time to catch the end of
Mac and Dev's conversation. Hearing her grandfather's
warning made Tanya smile, but it was unnecessary.

There was no way Devlin would hurt her. After what
she'd gone through over the holidays, no one could ever
wound her that way again.

Especially since she had no one to blame but herself.

Tanya reached for the old brass knob, but then remembered her hair still hung loose around her shoulders. Ignoring the fact it was still damp, she combed it back into
a ponytail and secured it with an elastic band from her
wrist, finishing the same moment that Mac knocked.

Tugging the door open, she saw the guilty looks on both
men's faces but said nothing, not letting on that she'd overheard them. "Hey, I just finished dressing and was about
to head over to the house to look for you two."

"Well, here we are." Mac offered a grin, reaching for
the screen door. "Ready whenever you are."

She stepped back and let them enter, watching Devlin's
face as he took in the cabin's interior, from the curtains
drawn against the afternoon sun to the soothing music
and lit candles. The air carried a hint of sandalwood and
vanilla, scents that Mac had said he liked the last time
she'd worked on him.

Her portable massage table, draped in a white sheet and a light blanket, was set up in the middle of the room. The best place for it, seeing how the cabin was a wide-open space with a kitchen along the back wall, a distressed table and chairs separating the cooking area from the living room.

His gaze roamed the room, flinching a moment when he noticed the tools of her trade, a hand-carved wooden box, lid open and packaged needles in sight, on the dining table. Then he moved on, pausing for a long moment on the old iron bed in the far corner, half hidden by a set of folding screens.

"Wow, the old cabin sure looks different from the last time I was here." Dev turned to face her. "I hardly recognize the place."

"You've stayed here before?"

"A time or two over the years." His mouth hitched into a half grin. "And you're right about that mattress. It is a bit lumpy."

Tanya's cheeks heated for the second time today. A heat that raced the length of her despite the fact she was dressed in simple beige lounge pants, a white tank top and a matching lightweight knit cardigan.

Suddenly she wanted to wrap the sides of the sweater across her chest, but she settled for crossing her arms. "Yes, well, I'm sure I'll get used to it."

"You should've said something. We can replace it if you want," Mac said.

"Don't be silly." She broke free of Dev's gaze and walked to the dining table, reaching out to rearrange the supplies that were already in perfect order. "I'm only going to be here for a couple of months."

"The old couch is pretty comfortable." Dev headed for the piece of furniture and Tanya turned to watch him, noticing how he favored his right leg even more than before. "But it looks too clean to sit on now."

"White is Tanya's favorite color. Once I knew she was coming to visit, I gave the walls and the kitchen cabinets a fresh coat of white paint," Mac said, walking over to join her. "Ursula helped with the decorating, everything from the white denim slip covers to the dishes."

"Let me guess. You like vanilla ice cream best?"

She dropped her arms. "Actually, I prefer oatmeal cookie chunk. And fixing this place up for me was totally unnecessary, but much appreciated."

"Not if you'd seen it in the before state." Dev's gaze wandered the length of her body. "Trust me, the after is a step up, even if it's a bit...unexciting."

"I prefer peaceful, tranquil." Tanya pushed the words from her mouth, refusing to believe her sudden breathlessness had anything to do with the interest she saw in Devlin's blue eyes.

Nerves, it was just nerves about working on Mac again.

She broke free from his gaze and dropped her hands, patting the table. "Mac, why don't you hop up here and stretch out on your back? Dev, you can grab a seat where you are. Unless you'd like to get a closer view of my work?"

Dev sat stiffly on the edge of the couch, the smile now gone from his face. "This is close enough."

Crossing to the kitchen sink, Tanya washed her hands again. When she got back to Mac, she found he'd already folded back the legs of his sweatpants before stretching out. Tucking the sheets and blanket around him, she left his lower legs and arms free.

"I'm going to talk as I go like the first time we did this, so Dev can understand what's going on." She offered Mac a smile, reaching for a needle packet from the box. "Ready to start?"

Mac flexed his fingers and then relaxed them across his stomach. "Ready."

She looked up, centering her gaze on Dev. "I have no idea how much you know about acupuncture—"

His brows drew down into a sharp V. "You get stuck with lots of needles."

"Well, not 'lots,' but let me back up a moment. Chinese medicine believes there are opposing forces, known as yin and yang, inside the body. When the forces are balanced, the body and the spirit are healthy. What helps to create this balance is an energy, a life force, called qi, which sounds like chee, but is spelled q-i. Qi flows through the body on a series of paths. When a path is obstructed, and in turn that force is blocked, illness can occur."

"Is this where I start to call you Obi-Wan?"

Tanya smiled. "The point of acupuncture is that by using pressure on specific points within these paths, it will release any barriers that are hindering the flow of qi, which in turn will allow the body to heal. Make sense?"

He didn't look convinced. "If you say so."

"Yeah, I thought it was a bunch of hocus-pocus at first, too." Mac turned his head and looked at Dev. "Now I'm a believer."

Tanya saw the doubt in Dev's eyes but continued, holding up the small packet in her hand. "Inside here is one needle. They are solid, hair thin and individually wrapped for sterilization. They are only used once and then tossed."

Dev went visibly pale when she ripped open the sealed paper around the needle.

Dropping her hands to Mac's lower leg, she held the needle between her index finger and thumb, out of Dev's sight, while using her other hand to locate the first puncture location below his knee.

"Okay, here we go." She looked at Mac. "Take a breath in…"

He did as instructed and after a quick tap on the end of the needle, it was in place.

"I thought this was to help Mac with the arthritis in his hands," Dev said, his voice a bit rough. "Why are you sticking him in his legs?"

"There are almost two thousand acupuncture points on the human body and each one has a different effect on the qi. I've already mapped out the specific positions needed to help Mac find relief and yes, there are quite a few located in each hand as well as other areas of his body."

"How long does he have to lie there like a human pincushion?"

"We did twenty minutes the past couple of times, but since it's been a while I think we'll go with a half hour today." She had another needle and location ready on the same leg. "Another breath in, Mac."

A quick glance up told her Dev was still watching, but his coloring had gone an even whiter shade of pale. "You okay over there?"

"Yeah, I'm fine."

"You might feel better if you stretched out on the couch—"

"I said I'm fine."

He wasn't. Tanya could see that plainly, from his coloring to the way he sat hunched forward, his hands clasped tightly between his knees, but she continued to work.

Keeping her tone light and even, she explained each step while keeping her attention on Mac, making sure her grandfather knew when she was going to insert each needle until he had a total of eight, two in each leg and two in each hand.

"Okay, now we move onto what is known as 'Eight

Ghosts,' which is the web area between each finger. Very helpful for those who suffer from pain and numbness in the fingers." Tanya completed one hand, then reached for the last set of needles. "Mac, maybe you can explain to Dev what sensations you are feeling as I finish up?"

"I would, but he's disappeared."

Tanya's head jerked up. Her gaze shot to the empty couch and then to Mac. "What? Where is he? What happened?"

"He was messing with his phone a moment ago, but as soon as you mentioned the between-the-fingers thing, he headed for the door."

Surprised that she hadn't heard him leave, Tanya tried to see if Dev was really gone or just outside on the porch getting some fresh air.

"Go."

She looked back at Mac. "What?"

"Go check on him. I'll be fine here."

"Not until your treatment is complete." She concentrated on inserting the final needles and then made sure Mac was comfortable. "Are you going to be okay?"

"I've got no plans to move an inch until you tell me I can." Mac grinned. "You better hightail it after him. He's moving slow, but he could be in his Jeep and halfway home by now."

Tanya crossed the room, slipped on a pair of wedge flip-flops and headed for the door. She left, leaving the inside door open in case her grandfather called out. She spotted Dev in a red Jeep parked at the hangar, the engine coming to life just as she made it to the passenger-side window.

"I understand, sweetie. I'll be there in a few minutes." Dev spoke into his phone. "Have I ever let you down? Hey, stop laughing."

She should step away and let him continue his conversation with his lady friend in private, but the moment Tanya moved he looked her way, doing a classic double take when he saw her.

"Gotta go, Abby. Driving and talking on a cell phone isn't a good thing. Especially when driving a stick." Dev ended the call, dropping his phone into the cup holder between the seats.

"Sorry, I didn't mean to eavesdrop." Tanya noticed his skin tone was back to normal, even though she could still see discomfort radiating from the deep creases around his eyes. "Mac noticed you left the cabin pretty fast toward the end. He wanted me to check on you."

"No need. I'm fi—"

"Fine. Yeah, you've said that already." Not that she believed him. "So, I take it you've decided that you're not interested in acupuncture."

"Guess I'm not brave or crazy." He grabbed the cowboy hat from the passenger seat and settled it on his head. "At least not enough to let you stick me."

She should be happy he was turning her down. Getting involved with Devlin during her stay in Destiny would be a crazy decision on her part, but the healer in her wanted desperately to ease the pain he wore like a heavy overcoat. "Does that mean you aren't interested in my help?"

"Oh, I'm interested." He flashed her that same wide smile that had called her to his side at the roulette wheel ten years ago. "I'm very interested."

Chapter Four

"For someone who said last week he was interested in my help, you don't seem to be trying very hard."

Dev tightened his grip on his fork and stabbed at the mound of mashed potatoes on his plate, but kept his tone light as he shot Tanya a quick wink from his side of the booth. "Well, I'm a little out of practice. Don't worry, it'll come back to me."

She rewarded him with the beginnings of a smile, but he still read concern—no, more like pity, in her gaze. "I'm talking about your physical therapy session this morning."

Yeah, he knew that.

Despite the fact he'd just about passed out watching her stick his buddy with a dozen or so needles, he'd told her he still wanted to work with her. But she'd insisted on meeting with Pete, his physical therapist, first, so she'd gone with him to a session today.

"And you pretty much glossed over what happened

after the accident and how hurt you really were. Pete filled in the details for me."

Dev shrugged and tried not to grimace at the soreness radiating through his shoulders and back. Hell, he was one giant wall of hurt after being stretched, pulled and twisted for sixty agonizing minutes.

Great way to start a Monday morning.

Not to mention the ride back to Destiny. He probably should've taken her up on her offer to grab lunch while they were in Laramie, but he'd figured the stretch behind the wheel would give his body more time to recover. Yeah, bad decision. He was stiff as a board.

And not in a good way.

"After eight months, it's been talked about enough."

She leaned forward, keeping her voice low despite the fact that Sherry's Diner, a popular place to eat in Destiny, was pretty much empty. "What you went through was horrible, but you've come such a long way since last summer. Why are you giving up now?"

Refusing to give that question any serious consideration, Dev mimicked her posture, bringing their faces close together over their half-eaten meals. He threw in one of his famous grins for good measure. "Who said anything about giving up? Maybe I was just waiting for you to come to the rescue."

"Except you're not interested in anything I specialize in." Tanya straightened and reached for her iced tea. "Other than a massage, of course."

Hmm, strike one for charm. "Couldn't be any worse than the beating I took today."

"Considering it's the first therapy appointment you've kept in the past three weeks, I'd say you're lucky you walked out of the clinic at all."

She was right on both counts. If he tried to stand up

now he'd probably fall flat on his face. As it was, he'd had to use to the cane just to keep upright in the parking lot.

"Pete also said you refuse to take any pain medication."

Now it was Dev's turn to sit back, his gaze glued to the table, certain he'd failed in keeping his discomfort off his face as the fire raced from his hip to his knee. "That's right."

"At all?"

He nodded, then looked up at her, not surprised by the disbelief in her eyes.

Giving the green light for Pete to share his medical records with Tanya had meant she'd learn that little tidbit about him, and he'd been waiting for her to bring it up. He figured now was as good a time as any for a discussion he'd had too many times to count in the past eight months with everyone from doctors to his folks.

"But why?"

Dev was glad they had scored one of the booths in the far corner of the diner. Not that it had prevented a few people from stopping by to say hello, lie to him that he looked good and force him to introduce Tanya.

Now he was glad for another reason, even though what he was about to say was certainly no secret in town.

"Because I'm an alcoholic."

Her eyebrows rose even higher until they disappeared beneath the fringe of bangs, her doubtful expression replaced with a look of pure surprise.

She didn't know.

He hadn't been sure if Mac had told her how the two of them had met and become friends since Dev had run out on the old man's pincushion session last Wednesday.

"I was twenty-seven when I finally got sick and tired of being a highly functioning drunk and joined AA," he continued. "Eight years ago this summer."

"Is that where you met Mac?"

"At the very first meeting. Of course, it took me almost a year of still being stupid and denying I actually had a drinking problem before I finally got with the program. Mac was always there for me. Still is."

Tanya's gaze dropped to her plate. She suddenly seemed very interested in her ketchup-laden fries. "It took Mac... my grandfather years to admit he had a problem."

"Didn't you say you once lived with him?"

"I was just a baby when my father took off and my mom and I had to move in with Mac. They used to have some real knock-down, drag-out fights about his drinking."

Trying to imagine a child living in that type of environment had Dev reaching for his ice water, his throat suddenly tight. "Is that why you moved when you were eight?"

She jerked her head up.

"Yeah, I've got a pretty good memory."

Tanya stared at him for a moment, and then gave in with a soft humph and looked away. Before he could ask her about it, she shook her head.

"One night my mom just threw everything we had into a couple of suitcases and we took off. I guess she couldn't take it anymore. I remember her saying Mac probably wouldn't even notice we were gone for at least a week."

"And you stayed gone for twenty-three years."

Tanya pulled in a deep breath then slowly released it. "Yes, we did. Thankfully, Mac finally got the help he needed, even though it took him another ten years. He found my mom not long after that—something to do with making amends—but it wasn't until last year we reconnected as a family."

"I think Mac's pretty happy about that and the fact

you're here," Dev said, then grinned. "And not just so you can practice your voodoo magic on him."

"Ah, which brings us back to working together and my original question about why you aren't taking any pain medication during your recovery."

She was a smart woman. At least he'd thought so. "Isn't it obvious?"

Tanya stared at him for a moment, tilting her head to one side. The action caused her straight, shiny hair, pulled back into a high ponytail, to slide over one shoulder. Damn, that was sexy. "You were afraid of your addiction finding a new vice."

Like he thought, smart. "Scared more of that than the possibility of losing a limb. Although that idea scared the crap out of me at the time, as well."

"When did you make this decision? If you don't mind me asking."

He didn't mind. Why should he? Lord knew, he'd been asked that question many times. "I don't remember being rescued. Okay, that's not exactly true. I do remember when the search team found me and my brother. Lucid moments were few and far between for me during the time we were lost, but I knew I'd been busted up pretty bad."

This was where the memories collided with reality.

"I thought… I could've sworn I told the EMTs I didn't want to be drugged, but I learned later I'd been in and out of consciousness most of that day. The next thing I knew I woke up in a hospital and had already had the first surgery to repair my leg. It was then I made it clear I wanted nothing that would take away the pain. The nurses thought I was nuts."

"I can imagine."

"I think I yanked out my IV tubing a few times…

every time I started feeling numb…lost in la-la land." Dev paused when the waitress stopped by and cleared away their dishes, waiting until she was gone before he went on. "It wasn't until my folks came in… Well, they knew I was serious. Then we got the doctors onboard."

"The pain must've been excruciating."

"It was a rough road. I had three more surgeries to deal with my two broken arms and a bad infection that developed in my leg. That kept me in the hospital for a long time. After a lot of discussions, I ended up taking mostly NSAIDs, nonsteroidal anti-inflammatory drugs, but even those I weaned myself off as soon as I could. Hell, I rarely take anything even for a headache."

She looked at him for a long moment and Dev felt his skin grow hot under her scrutiny. Outside of his family, medical team and Mac, Tanya was the first person he'd talked to about this part of his recovery.

"Is this refusal to take pain medication the reason you've been slack on your physical therapy?"

"Well, it sure hurts like hell afterwards." Dev held up his hands, unable to truly spread his arms wide. "Usually I just 'Duke' it out."

"I'm sorry, what does that mean?"

"You know, the Duke? John Wayne? Take it like a man?" Dev laughed and dropped his hands back to the table when she rolled her eyes at him. "Hey, I'm doing okay. Might not be a hundred percent, but considering where I started…"

"And no one ever offered alternative methods for dealing with the pain?"

"You mean like yours?"

"Yes. There's quite a variety of disciplines out there. Acupuncture being one, of course, but there's also self-hypnosis, Reiki, meditation, aromatherapy or even electrical nerve stimulation."

"Well, some of those were talked about, but—"

"You're not a fan of unconventional medicine." Tanya crossed her arms, propping them on the edge of the table. "So tell me again why you want to work with me?"

Now it was Dev's turn to stare as silence stretched between them.

Damn, she was pretty. Dressed in cream-colored slacks and a simple white cotton sweater, she looked very professional.

He guessed that was the point of today's appointment, but he missed the revealing, body hugging outfits he'd seen her in last week.

He took in her peaches-and-cream skin, beautiful eyes with long, dark lashes and mouth that begged to be kissed.

His body responded to where his thoughts were headed, and why not, when the rest of him was tight and hurting.

"I'm not really sure," he finally answered, deciding to keep his thoughts to himself. "You're obviously skilled in your chosen profession and you believe in what you do. You already know needles are out, but you must have some other tricks up your sleeve. Besides, I trust you."

An easy smile came to her lips. "You say that like it's a surprise."

He chuckled. "Yeah, I guess it is, although I don't really know why I trust you. Who knows? Maybe this whole thing between us was meant to be. I just can't get over how you seem very familiar."

"Do I?"

Two simple words, but Dev had noticed how her smile changed. Still there, but it wasn't as easy and relaxed as before. "I know it sounds strange, but it's almost as if we've met before. In a previous life, maybe?"

* * *

Before Tanya could respond, their waitress appeared again with their bill and flashed her pretty green eyes at Dev despite the fact she looked like she was barely out of high school.

Thankful for the timely interruption, Tanya took a moment to do her own relaxation technique. A few deep breaths and a mental image of a field of wildflowers slowed her heart from the frantic pounding that had started the moment Dev had fallen silent when she'd pushed for an answer about why he wanted to work with her.

Dev's aversion to medication wasn't something new to her. She'd successfully treated others with substance abuse problems, but those patients had been looking for and willing to take on alternative methods.

Dev wanted to work with her because he trusted her.

An important reason, granted, but was he using her profession and his accident as a way to spend more time with her? Was he finally remembering their night together in Reno?

Dev handed over cash, including a generous tip, and then turned his charming smile away from the waitress and back to her. "So, where were we?"

Changing the subject, that's where. "I thought we were splitting the bill for lunch."

"No worries. I can afford it."

His casual tone had her fingers tightening around her glass. "Despite my grandfather's monetary offer last week, I do have a few dollars in my wallet."

"That's not what I meant." Dev placed a hand over hers. "You can get the bill next time."

Tanya pulled in another deep breath and relaxed. "Who says there's going to be a next time?"

"Oh, I'm sure there will be. We're just getting to know each other."

Thinking this was a great time for a trip to the ladies' room, she opened her mouth to ask for directions when a low, deep voice suddenly filled the air.

"Hey, Dev, imagine running into you here. And with a pretty girl, no less." A dark-haired man with black-framed glasses walked up to the booth. "Rumor had it you were getting back into the swing of things."

Tanya easily picked up the resemblance between the newcomer and Devlin. There were six Murphy brothers. She wondered which one this was.

He wore a crisp business suit, the only flaw being the striped tie shoved into the jacket's breast pocket. His fancy attire contrasted with Dev's, who was again wearing jeans, a cotton button-down shirt and sneakers instead of cowboy boots.

"Shut up, Liam."

The man didn't seem bothered by Dev's rude greeting. He turned to Tanya with a smile almost identical to Dev's and held out his hand. "Liam Murphy. And you are?"

"Tanya Reeves." She placed her hand in his, returning his greeting. "Nice to meet you."

"So where did you meet my brother?" Liam released her, then removed his glasses and stuck them in the same pocket as his tie. "Please tell me it was someplace nice... like the library."

"Tanya is Mac's granddaughter. She's here for a visit."

"I didn't know Mac had a granddaughter. Welcome to Destiny, Tanya." Liam motioned for permission to sit next to her. "Mind if I join you two?"

Tanya glanced at Devlin. He didn't seem happy at his brother's self-invite, but she liked the easygoing mischief in the other man's blue eyes. They didn't have the icy cerulean coloring of Dev's, more like the deep navy of the creek that ran through town.

He was a handsome guy, but there was no zing when she looked at him.

No big surprise. Men were off her radar for the foreseeable future.

Which didn't explain the heart-pounding reaction she seemed to get on a regular basis from the man across from her.

Why was that? Ah, yes. His "you seem familiar" comment.

Not wanting to get back to that conversation, she scooted over to give the man room to sit. "Oh, please do. This is my first time back in Destiny in years."

"So how is it you've already hooked up with my brother?"

"Oh, we haven't— We aren't…hooked up."

Dev's features tightened, but she didn't know if that was from him being in pain or worried at what she might say. Not that she had any idea how to describe what was going on between the two of them at the moment.

"We actually just met a few days ago—"

"Out at Mac's place." Dev cut in. "How was your conference in Chicago?"

"Oh, you know. Busy and crowded, much like the city, but the eats were good and we did a fair amount of business." Liam waved off the waitress when she started toward the booth. "I met an actor from Scotland or Ireland, I can't remember which, at one of the conference's black-tie events. He was an Avenger or a superhero—someone like that. Anyway, Ian saw the spread that architecture magazine did on Bobby Winslow's place."

"Bobby Winslow?" Tanya asked. "The three-time champion race-car driver?"

"One and the same. Although he retired a couple of

years ago after a bad crash," Liam said. "You a racing fan?"

"One of my girlfriends back in Colorado Springs is… or was." Tanya smiled, remembering Kate's obsession with the handsome driver. "She's still trying to find a new driver to switch her loyalties to, not to mention her affections. Your company built a log home for him?"

"Not just a home, a mansion. Over ten thousand square feet, five bedrooms, an indoor pool and an elevator," Liam said. "The foreigner wants one twice that size."

"Fascinating," Dev deadpanned.

"It could be, considering the location of the build. I've got to get in touch with Bobby and Leann to see if they'd be interested in showing off their place to the guy. And big brother Nolan is going to really enjoy working up these plans."

"Well, if you can squeeze me into your busy work schedule I'd like to talk to you, too."

"Sure. Being the big-time movie star this guy is, he'll definitely want a state-of-the-art security system." Liam looked back at Tanya and grinned. "I'm sorry. Are we boring you with all this shop talk?"

"No, I find your family's company interesting. Mac and I went out for a drive after church yesterday and he showed me a lot of the homes and businesses you built."

"You should have Dev bring you by the compound. We've got a few model homes, the company headquarters and the places we've built for our brothers, all log built, of course. Dev can give you a grand tour and show off his office. The man has more computer screens over his desk than Bill Gates—"

"I wasn't talking about work or a new customer," Dev interrupted his brother, "and you know it."

Liam's easy smile slipped and a muscle along his jaw

twitched. "Yeah, I know. I called into the office after I landed in Cheyenne. Dad answered the phone."

"I want to talk to you and Bryant."

"Well, Bry and Laurie decided to extend their stay in the city for a few more days. Can it wait until they get back?"

"Oh, sure." Dev's casual tone defied the fierce look in his eyes. "Why go over the same topic twice?"

Tanya's gaze shot between the two men, the tension in the air palpable. Dev wasn't happy with his brother about something. She wondered if it had anything to do with his injuries, or perhaps his lackadaisical attitude over his physical therapy. His brother did say he was back to work, but—

"Well, I better run. A ton of paperwork awaits me at the office." Liam slapped a hand to the table and pushed to his feet. "I'll see you at home later?"

Dev gave a quick nod. "Count on it."

The man turned to Tanya, his expression relaxed again. "Tanya, it was nice to meet you. Hope to see you again. In fact, if my twin here backs out on giving you the tour, just stop on by. As the company president, I can give you a personal tour."

A low growl—or was that Dev clearing his throat?—came from the other side of the table. She looked at him, but he only grabbed his glass of water and took a long drink.

"Ah, thanks." She looked back at Liam. "I'll keep that in mind."

The man walked away and Tanya turned back to Devlin, noticing he seemed more relaxed now that it was just the two of them again.

"Twin?" she asked. "You don't look that much alike."

"Irish twins. Our birthdays are only eleven months apart."

"You were close growing up?"

"We fought like cats and dogs over everything from toys to girls." Dev set his glass back on the table with a thunk and reached for his cane. "And for the past three months he's been more nursemaid than boss to me. You ready to get out of here?"

He obviously was, so Tanya nodded, grabbed her purse and scooted out of the booth. Turning to make sure Dev got to his feet okay was a natural reaction, but the scowl on his face told her he didn't appreciate her doing so.

"We've been sitting for a while," she said, keeping her voice low. "I wanted to make sure you were okay."

"Meaning you wanted a front row seat when I took a face plant?" Dev gripped the cane's curved handle so tightly his knuckles turned white. "Maybe I should have let Liam stick around to witness that. Not that he hasn't seen me in worse moments."

"I won't let you fall."

Dev went still and stared at her. His eyes locked with hers and Tanya could almost see the wheels turning inside his head.

What was he thinking?

"Thanks," he finally said. "But I'm okay. Let's go."

They exited the diner and headed for the nearby parking lot. They were just about to get into his Jeep when they heard Dev's name called out, this time from across the street.

He stopped and turned, a muttered curse falling from his lips. "Just what I don't need right now."

Tanya looked past Dev and saw two men and a woman, all wearing matching dark blue outfits, heading their way.

"I'm guessing you know them?" she asked.

"Yeah, they're friends...and former coworkers."

"They used to work for your family's business?"

Dev blew out a breath. He then angled his body so he could rest against the side of his vehicle, taking some of the pressure off his leg. "They're members of the Destiny Fire Department."

Another surprise today. "You're a firefighter?"

Dev reached for the sunglasses he'd tucked into a shirt pocket when they'd first sat down to eat. Before he shoved them into place, Tanya saw a wounded expression in his eyes, ten times worse than what had been there when he'd first come out of the changing room at the clinic after his tortuous physical therapy session.

"Was," he said quietly. "I was a firefighter."

Chapter Five

Two days later, Devlin pulled into an empty spot in the parking lot of the Destiny Fitness Center, shut off the Jeep's engine and sat for a moment, admiring the view. The almost two-thousand-square-foot building was less than a year old, but it looked like it'd been a part of Destiny since its founding in the late 1800s.

For a town this small, the place was impressive, with full-service locker rooms, separate cardio and strength training areas, a calendar full of fitness classes and two indoor pools.

The center had been the last project Dev had worked on before the crash.

He'd supervised the installation of the high tech security system he'd designed as best he could from his hospital bed, but had taken a pass on the grand opening back in January, even though he'd been home by then.

With both arms in casts from his elbows to his wrists

and a leg he'd still been learning how to work again, he'd quickly become a hermit.

At least until last week.

As part of the building contract, the entire Murphy family had received complimentary yearlong memberships to the center. His brothers raved about the place, and his folks, officially retired from the family business, were here almost every day.

Which is why Dev hadn't told anyone about his appointment this morning with Tanya.

He thought back to Monday afternoon when they'd run into his former coworkers. He had to admit he'd been surprised she hadn't heard about his volunteer work with the fire department.

Mac hadn't told her about him being in AA, he got that, but he'd figured his buddy had at least told her the rest of it. Then again, the man wasn't too happy about Dev's interest in his granddaughter, so Dev guessed he hadn't come up in conversation much during Tanya's first few days in town.

Or maybe she hadn't been interested enough to ask any questions about him.

Before that thought could take hold, his friends had joined them and he'd introduced her. Then he gave non-committal answers to their questions about his recovery and when he was going to return to the department.

By the time he and Tanya were alone again, he'd been so stiff from standing there, it'd taken all of his strength to crawl into the driver's seat.

That's when she'd told him his volunteer work with the fire department had given her the perfect idea for how to help him.

He'd asked if she planned to set him on fire, earning

him a husky laugh that made him feel like he'd just won the lottery.

Then she'd said, "Just the opposite—aquatic therapy."

Dev had pointed out he could barely walk. How did she expect him to swim? But she'd only said he wouldn't actually be swimming and to just leave everything to her.

After dropping her off, he'd done some research online, finding out this type of therapy was popular because people felt weightless in the water and didn't have to worry about falling and getting hurt. He still hadn't been too sure about this idea.

Hell, he'd thought about calling her back and canceling the whole thing, but then he realized if he was going to be in swim trunks Tanya would be similarly attired.

And that made it almost worth it.

What could it hurt to give it a try?

Grabbing the duffel bag from the passenger seat, Dev got out of his Jeep before he let his mind fully form the mental image of the sexy brunette wearing a one-piece bathing suit.

He debated leaving the cane behind, but figured he'd better bring it along, considering how much he'd needed the damn thing after Monday's PT session.

He enjoyed the coolness of the spring morning as he crossed the parking lot. It was supposed to get quite warm later, though, especially for May 1 in Wyoming. The grounds surrounding the building were in full bloom with native wildflowers, courtesy of his sister-in-law, Fay, the local florist who also did landscaping.

His admiration for the building increased tenfold when he entered the reception area, seeing for the first time how his brother's architectural plans had come to life in the airy, open space. The log walls were lighter in color inside and lots of floor-to-ceiling windows let in plenty of sunshine. Plotted plants and comfortable furniture filled out the area, making it warm and welcoming.

"Hi, you must be Devlin Murphy." An older woman, her gray hair pulled up in a bun that made her look like a skinny Mrs. Claus, stood behind the front counter. "Ms. Reeves said to expect you this morning."

"That's me." He looked around again, this time searching for Tanya. "Is she here yet?"

"Oh, yes. She's probably changing. Here's your membership packet for the center. If you'll come with me, I'll show you to the locker room."

Dev shoved the packet into the side pocket of his duffel and followed her through the expansive building, noticing through interior glass walls there were already a number of people working out on various pieces of equipment.

"What time do you open in the mornings?" he asked.

"Five-thirty during the week." She looked back at him over her shoulder. "Seven a.m. on weekends."

Great. Was there going to be an audience for this little experiment?

He'd remembered reading that the center had two indoor pools. Maybe Tanya had reserved one of them for the hour she'd said it would take to do the therapy?

"The general member's locker rooms are farther down, but I was told to bring you to the private area used by the owners and their guests." His guide paused outside a simple door and quickly entered a code on the keypad. "Once you get inside you'll see the entrance for the men on the left. You can choose any of the empty changing rooms and then just follow the signs, and your nose, to the pool area."

Dev thanked her and entered, impressed again with the attention to detail in the men's locker room.

There were six private changing rooms, each with its own toilet, sink and shower, as well as a common area outfitted with the same stylish furniture he'd seen out front and a refreshment area.

He checked his watch, noticing he was running late. Entering one of the rooms, he quickly changed into a pair of dark blue board shorts, catching his reflection in the mirror.

The twenty-five pounds he'd lost since the accident was noticeable, and while the surgeons had been masters at stitching him up every time, he'd always have the surgical and metal pin scars on three of his four limbs.

Dev dug into his bag for a T-shirt and pulled it on. The nylon fabric wasn't skintight, but it hugged his body from his shoulders to his waist, the three-quarter sleeves coming down to his elbows.

He wasn't sure if he'd leave it on for the entire session, but for someone who'd always prided himself on keeping his body in top physical condition, it bruised his ego to see how different he looked now.

Grabbing one of the center's towels from a nearby rack, he slipped into his flip-flops and left the changing room, pausing to switch the sign on the door from vacant to occupied since his street clothes were in there.

Once out in the hallway, he noticed a doorway that led from the ladies' locker area and headed for the pool, the faint smell of chlorine not as strong as he'd expected it to be.

He reached for the handle on the glass door, the moisture clinging to the glass not entirely obscuring his view.

What he'd feared was true. A crowd. He quickly counted at least a dozen people standing around on the pool deck with another smaller group already in the waist-deep water.

All female and all old enough to be his grandmother. *What the hell was this?*

His gaze locked with Tanya's through the glass and she excused herself from the women she was talking to and started for him.

No turning back.

He pushed open the door and stepped inside, the sound of the female chatter reverberating inside the warm, humid space.

"I know this probably isn't what you expected." Tanya spoke before he could say a word. "Our reservation time for the workout pool was double-booked with the Wet Nanas. I only found out when I got out here, but this might be a good thing, if you're willing."

Willing was the only word that came through loud and clear.

The rest of what she was saying came out as a muffled echo because all Dev could concentrate on was her outfit.

Or lack thereof.

She wore a long-sleeved, lightweight sweatshirt that clung to her curves. Zippered, it covered her from her cleavage to the tops of her thighs. Common sense told him she wore a bathing suit of some sort beneath the clingy material, but the sight of her long legs—and her toenails painted bright red—had him thinking thoughts wholly inappropriate for the moment.

Like watching her slowly pull that zipper downward.

Thank goodness for the towel he held at his waist.

"Dev? Did you hear what I said?"

She gave his arm a gentle squeeze and a hot flare of awareness flashed through him. Her eyes widened for a moment before she released him, but he knew she'd felt that same electric charge he did.

He offered her his best, charming smile. "No, I'm sorry. I was a bit distracted by my…" pausing, he couldn't resist another leisurely exploration of the perfection in front of him "…surroundings."

"Well, the class starts right now." Tanya backed up a few steps as she brushed her fingers across the front of her sweatshirt.

Huh?

"Are you aware there's a group of bingo-playing grandmas into water aerobics who consider themselves your personal fan club?"

His lust-filled fog was slowly dissipating as her words sank in. "Fan club? What are you talking about?"

"Devlin!"

Moments later, Dev was in fact surrounded by a group of familiar ladies, regulars at the weekly bingo nights run by the town's fire department.

Of course, they looked a whole lot different without their clothes on, and there went his need for the towel. Keeping his gaze entirely on their faces more than erased his body's first reaction to seeing Tanya this morning.

"Oh, we've missed you so much at bingo!"

"Wednesdays just haven't been the same without you calling out the numbers for us!"

"You look wonderful, dear!"

"So glad to see you up and moving! You just have to join us this morning!"

The ladies' words jumbled together, their excitement growing until Dev finally held up a hand and they all quieted down. He looked over their heads and found Tanya standing there, watching him with a bemused smile on her pretty face.

"Ah, thank you, ladies. It's good to see all of you, too." He had to admit their enthusiasm was nice, but while he had enjoyed their banter and harmless flirting, it didn't mean he was interested in getting into the pool with this crowd. "It seems I've disrupted your class, so I'll go and let you—"

"Oh, no! You're going to join us." The leader of the group, Esther Dimpleton, gray curls and huge purple earrings bouncing together in perfect rhythm, cut off his escape, both physically and verbally. "We've already cleared it with that charming young lady friend of yours. She is going to keep an eye on you because as we all know you are still recovering from that dreadful accident, but we promise to take it easy on you."

Knowing it was better to give in than try to win a losing argument, Devlin smiled at the ladies and gestured to the pool. They all cheered and headed for the water.

Dev headed for Tanya.

"Do you have any idea how much ammunition my brothers are going to get out of this? I'll be hearing about this moment until I'm as old as these ladies." He handed her the towel, staring at the mesh-and-rubber-soled shoes she in turn handed to him. "What are those?"

"Water shoes. They will give you traction in the pool. They should fit."

Dev took the shoes and moved to a nearby bench to sit and put them on.

"How are you feeling this morning?" Tanya asked, joining him but keeping the towel a barrier between their bodies.

"Now's a great time to ask that question."

"I asked you earlier, but you didn't seem to be listening."

He caught sight again of her painted toes. "I was distracted. Red is a good color on you."

He grinned when she tried to tuck her feet out of sight.

"Listen, I want to cover a few things before the class gets started. The water aerobics usually run about forty-five minutes, but you don't have to stay in the pool the whole time," Tanya said. "After the warm-up, the instructor will lead the group in a series of moves, like arm and leg swings, side bends, front and side kicks, but only do what you can. Don't push yourself."

Yeah, like he was going to let a bunch of old ladies show him up.

"The water temperature will be warmer than what you might be used to, but this pool was designed specifically for these kinds of classes and your muscles will stay relaxed. The depth of the water goes from three-and-a-half feet on the right end to four-and-a-half feet on the left. You should go for the deeper end because of your height. I've already told the ladies that you'll stand in the last row near the pool's edge."

Dev looked at her, annoyed at what she was implying. "Why? In case I need to grab hold to keep from drowning?"

"Yes."

Her frank answer defused his irritation instantly. He looked away from her and out at the grandmas already warming up in the water.

Tanya was probably right.

He'd never done anything like this before, but most of the ladies had at least thirty years on him and some looked as if all it'd take to knock them over was a stiff wind.

How hard could this be?

"I told the ladies you being in the back was best because of your height. You wouldn't want to block any of them from seeing the instructor."

"Thanks." Then a thought came to him. "Wait, you're not taking the class, too?"

She shook her head and reached for a nearby clipboard. "Normally I would be right there in the water next to you directing your session, but this way I can track the movements you do, the number of reps and make notes for the next time."

All this and he'd still have no idea what she wore beneath that sweat jacket when he was done.

Life was not fair.

Poor Devlin. Those old ladies kicked his ass.

He was still in shoulder-deep water, leaning against the pool's edge. His breathing was more even now that the class was over, but Tanya could see the discomfort and fatigue on his face. Still, he spoke with each of the ladies and made sure they got up the pool's ladder safely.

He was determined to be the last one out.

Tanya was proud at how he made it through the entire class, even if her notes reflected how his range of motion had narrowed considerably toward the end.

That was good.

He'd worked hard, probably harder than if it had just been the two of them. Determined not to be shown up by a bunch of grandmothers, he'd kept going. She'd monitored him closely, using slight hand gestures to remind him to keep track of his heart rate and control his breathing.

She was proud of him.

"Is the coast clear?"

Even though Devlin and she were now alone in the pool area, she made an exaggerated effort to look around while grabbing his towel from the nearby bench.

"Yes, I think it's safe to get out of the water," she said in a hushed whisper.

"Very funny." Dev straightened to his full height until he stood waist deep, the water sluicing off his shoulders making the material of his shirt cling to his body like a second skin. "Damn, I'm hurting."

Tanya tried, but it was impossible to look away.

She had read in his medical records about how much weight he'd lost in the past eight months, but the man was still the image of perfection. He had a naturally tan skin tone and the pale patchwork of scars on his lower arms and leg only stood as a testament of what he'd survived.

"Tanya?"

She blinked, realizing he'd gotten out of the pool and was standing in front of her. Oh, great therapist she was! Not even aware of him climbing the ladder!

Or the fact that he'd peeled off his T-shirt, taken the towel from her hands and was busy drying off the hard planes of his chest and abdomen.

Yummy.

"Are you ready to get dressed?" he asked, a slight smile on his lips. "It's a bit cold now that I'm out of the water."

"Oh, right. Of course, let's get you changed." She turned away to gather her stuff, silently bemoaning her choice of words. "Um, I mean, let's both of us get changed."

Dev turned and started for the doorway that led to the private locker rooms, his movements slow and measured. She fell into step next to him, reaching to open the glass door before he could.

He paused and looked at her, his mouth pressed into a hard line. She didn't know if that was from his sore ego or sore muscles, but she ignored him and stepped aside, waiting for him to go ahead of her.

It was quieter here in the hallway—just the sound of their footsteps and Dev's uneven breathing as he walked in front of her.

"Are you okay?" she asked. "I know you got a good workout in the pool—"

"I'm fine."

She rolled her eyes. They were back to "fine." They

were also almost to the entrance to the men's locker room. "You know, you're going to have to share a few more details than just 'fine' if we're going to work— Oh!"

Dev stumbled and fell into the door.

She dropped everything in her hands and reached for him, slipping underneath his arm to wrap herself around him. He braced his right arm against the wall and pulled her close with his left as his still-considerable bulk sank into her.

His body molded to hers and that sizzle they'd shared when she'd touched his arm earlier ran the length of both of them.

A powerful mix of pleasure and need, two things she'd been sure she'd never wanted or expected to feel again for a long time, exploded deep inside her.

"Dev…" His name came out in a sigh against his skin, her lips brushing the edge of his collarbone.

His hand moved low on her back, gathering the soft material of her sweat jacket in a tight grip until it inched up over her backside.

"Give me…give me a second."

She counted to ten, but then she had to see him. Tilting her head back caused her to bump into the wall.

Dev swore beneath his breath and then released his hold on the wall, his fingers tangling with her ponytail as he cupped her scalp.

His lips, warm and wet, brushed across her forehead and she gasped.

He swore again and a moment later crushed his mouth to hers.

Chapter Six

Oh, this man could still kiss.

She'd been young but far from innocent when she'd been kissed by Devlin Murphy the first time a decade ago.

Thanks to her wild and turbulent teenage years, Tanya had done her fair share of kissing long before her twenty-first birthday, which she'd celebrated a few months before that night with Dev.

Still, that night had been an anniversary of sorts for her.

After a yearlong, self-imposed abstinence from the male species, especially those she came in contact with as a showgirl at the Desert Kings Casino in Reno, Tanya had practically melted the moment the sexy cowboy gambler had backed her into the glass wall of the casino's elevator and took her mouth.

And here she was…melting again.

A soft moan escaped from her lips when he broke free for air. Seconds later he was back, and she was kissing him in return, as he pressed her against the wall with the length of his body.

The damp heat of his skin seemed to burn beneath her hands as she clung to his wide shoulders. Droplets of pool water fell from his hair to land on her closed eyelids and cheeks as he cradled her head in the palm of his hand.

He released her mouth to trail kisses along her jaw until he reached that spot just below her earlobe. She tilted her head to one side, giving his tongue access to her pulsing heartbeat at the same moment he released his hold on the back of her sweat jacket.

"I need…" His whispered words filled her ear while his fingers slid between their bodies, the back of his hand brushing across her breasts until he latched on to the zipper. "Need to know what you look like underneath this… Ah, dammit!"

Tanya's eyes flew open the moment he let go of her, his palms slamming into the wall on either side of her head.

She looked up and read the agony causing his handsome features to twist and contort into something ugly and pain filled.

"Where?" she demanded, her hands sliding down his arms to his elbows and then continuing toward his wrists. The muscles were tight and firm, but smooth. "Where is it?"

"Leg." The word came out with a low hiss as he clenched his jaw, the veins in his neck thick and pronounced as he arched his face toward the ceiling. "Right…leg."

Keeping her back to the wall, Tanya dropped to the floor, balancing on the balls of her feet for a moment before she knelt in front of him. Trailing her fingers over his leg, she searched for the source of his pain, starting up high beneath the bottom hem of his shorts.

Her fingertips caught on the scars, the long incision that

ran along his gluteus maximus to the back of his knee and the smaller individual ones from the metal screws that had held the bones together while they'd healed.

She worked her way downward until she reached his upper calf. Geez, the gastrocnemius muscle was twisted six ways to Sunday.

"Put your weight on your good leg."

"I am." Dev punched out the words, but he shifted anyway. "Yeah, you're close…ah, shhh-oot…you found it."

She had. The cramp was a massive one and she immediately went to work, pushing deep into the muscle. After a few minutes it started to give way, but not enough yet to relieve the pain, as was evident from the string of colorful phrases Dev whispered between short breaths.

"Slow your breathing," she commanded.

"I can't."

"Purse your lips."

"Excuse me?"

"Purse your lips," she repeated, not taking her eyes off his leg. "You know, pucker up like you're going to blow a…kiss."

"Yeah, that's not—that's not how I kiss. You should know that by now."

Yes, she did, many times over. "Do it anyway. Before you pass out on me."

"Ah, Tanya… Just let me sit down. You're not helping."

"Yes, I am, you just can't feel it yet." Moving her hands away from the muscle, she positioned the fingertips of one hand behind his knee, between the two ligaments located there, and then placed her other hand on the back of his ankle and applied even pressure.

A pain-filled groan rent the air around them. "You have to—have to stop whatever it is you're doing."

"I'm applying acupressure points to get rid of the leg

cramp." Tanya tested the strained muscle again. She could already feel the slackening in the fibers around his calf. "See? It's working. The pressure is releasing."

"No," his voice dropped to a husky level, "it's not."

"What are you talking about?" She looked up and found Dev, arms still braced against the wall, staring down at her.

Only the raw pain that had been in his eyes earlier had transformed into something even more dangerous.

Unrestrained desire.

He directed his gaze down to a certain part of his body and she followed his line of sight, finally noticing the tight stretch of his board shorts across the most intimate part of him.

"Oh."

"Yeah. Oh."

"Are you serious?" She looked back up at his face. "You've just experienced a leg cramp that would have most professional athletes curled up in a ball crying like a baby and you're thinking about sex?"

"Hey, the leg cramps happen all the time." He offered a smile that came off more like a grimace. "It's been almost a year since I've had sex."

A year? Really?

"Yes, really." He easily read the questions running through her head. "So, if you could—hell, I can't believe I'm actually saying this—if you could get up off your knees, I'd appreciate it."

She took a moment to test the muscle again, ignoring his muttered protest as she pressed, happy to find the area more relaxed now.

Rising, she braced one hand behind her, the other immediately going to Dev's waist when he tried to put weight on his injured leg and take a step back.

"Wait! What are you doing?"

"Trying to get away from you."

Ouch, that smarted a bit. She wrapped her arm around his waist anyway. "Let me help you."

One arm came down to rest across her shoulders. "Is that an offer?"

"Into the locker room." Tanya opened the door and kicked the items they'd both dropped inside and out of the way. Then they shuffled inside after she announced a female was entering and only silence greeted them. "Nice. This is set up just like the ladies' side. Which changing room is yours?"

Dev pointed to the closed door and they hobbled into the tiny space, Tanya staying right by him until Dev sank onto the bench.

He leaned his head back against the wall with a soft thud and closed his eyes. "Damn, it feels good to sit."

Tanya stood in front of him, studying his face. Tension still creased his forehead. "Let me take another look at your leg."

Dev's only movement was to fold his hands together and lay them in his lap. "Is that really necessary?"

"Yes."

"Yeah, I thought you'd say that. Maybe this will work better if I keep my eyes closed."

She shook her head, unable to decide if it was in response to his adolescent sexual innuendos or the fact she now had erotic scenarios dancing around inside her head. "Whatever rocks your world."

"Okay, saying things like that are definitely not helping." He grinned, but his eyes remained shut.

Tanya smiled, but then reminded herself she was working with him in a professional capacity and took a step back, not easy to do in the confined space.

Concentrating on the task at hand, she knelt again and examined his lower leg for several minutes, massaging the area with gentle pressure this time.

"The area is still warm to the touch, but the swelling has gone down."

"That's what you think."

He muttered the words beneath his breath, but she heard him anyway.

She sat back on her heels and sighed. "Dev…"

"I know, I'm sorry." He pulled in a deep breath, and then slowly released it. Placing his hands on the flat surface of the bench, he pushed back with his good leg, straightening his posture while keeping his injured leg outstretched.

He opened his eyes and looked at her. "Thank you… for the magic fingers. That cramp hurt like a son of a— Well, it hurt, and you got rid of that sucker faster than anyone else who's tried."

The sincerity in his words and gaze surprised her.

She got to her feet, automatically tugging the sweat jacket down over her hips. "You're welcome. You know, the cramping was probably caused by your muscles tensing—"

"Tell me about it."

"After being in the warm pool water for so long and then exposed to the cool air." She ignored his wisecrack and waved at the nearby glass-enclosed shower. "You should take a long, warm shower. It'll help you relax."

"I was thinking the same thing, but with the water temperature set a bit lower. Like arctic level. Now, about that kiss—"

"Don't worry about that." Tanya cut him off before he went any further. "It won't happen again."

His blue eyes flashed. "Like hell it won't."

"Dev, we're working together on your recovery and I've made it a policy not to get involved with my—" her tongue tripped up over her own lie "—with people I work with."

He stayed silent for a moment, and then crossed his arms over his chest, wincing at the movement. "Why?"

Tanya pulled her gaze from the play of muscles bunching in those magnificent arms and shoulders. "Why, what?"

"Why the policy? Most people don't have dating rules without a reason. Me? I've got two." He held up one hand, extending his fingers. "The first? No dating a girl who used to be with one of my brothers. Too messy. And two, no fix ups from my folks. That's a sure-fire recipe for disaster."

Tanya smiled, remembering how her mom would start many phone calls with how she'd found the "perfect" guy for her. "Your mother?"

"You'd think so, but no, it was my dad." Dev grinned and shook his head. "Don't ask. Just take my word for it that the night ended badly for many reasons, starting with the fact the young lady had a fondness for handcuffs and a leather-studded whip. How about you?"

Tanya pulled in a deep breath, shoving her hands into the jacket's pockets. Other than a few close friends and her mother, she hadn't talked about her recent romantic disaster with anyone.

Did it matter if she shared it with Dev? It's not like anything was going to change between them.

"I was involved with someone at the clinic where I used to work in Colorado Springs. We had been together for a few years, but when I—" she paused, pressing her lips together hard for a moment "—when I left my job back around Christmas, he ended the relationship, as well."

"Because you stopped working together?"

Oh, if it were only that simple. There was so much more to what happened between her and Ross, but she wasn't going to go into that now. "Because he was my boss."

"Oh. Yeah, well, I can see why that would make you a bit gun-shy."

Gun-shy, yes, but where were the familiar pangs of regret she usually had when talking about this? One would think it'd take longer than a few months to get over a four-year relationship, not to mention the hit her career and her pocketbook had taken when she left the clinic.

"Thank you for understanding."

"But there is an easy fix." Dev pushed to his feet. "You're fired."

Tanya concentrated on his movements, ready to step forward if needed, but he was steady even as he favored his one leg.

Then she realized what he'd just said.

Looking up at him, she studied his face, trying to gauge if he was joking. "You don't really want to fire me."

"No."

Releasing the breath she didn't even know she'd been holding, Tanya realized how much she did want to help Dev get over his injuries. If he'd only commit to his physical therapy and allow her to help in every way she could—

"But I really do want to kiss you again."

His simple words cut into her thoughts and reignited the heat between them.

If she was going to be honest, which had become her new policy since her life had gone topsy-turvy four months ago, she'd admit, if only to herself, kissing him again was what she wanted, too.

But wanting and having were two totally different things.

"That would not be a good idea. Especially for us."

Dev took a step forward. "I don't agree."

Her desire shifted into mild panic, and she took a step back but found herself up against a shelving unit filled with towels and bathing amenities. "Look, I'll admit that moment out in the hall was unavoidable. The two of us spending so much time together… It was inevitable we'd end up here, and that's my fault. I should've known better, considering our history, but once was more than enough—"

"Wait a minute, back up." Dev cut her off with a quick jerk of his hand. "Considering our history? What history?"

Oh, no.

Tanya bit down on her bottom lip. Had she really said that aloud?

Okay, she'd known that night in Reno was going to come to light eventually. Either the man would remember her—she'd hoped!—or she'd end up telling him.

Preferably as a "ha-ha, you won't believe this but…" kind of story over a shared coffee or a steaming cup of green tea, her preferred choice of morning beverage.

But not like this.

Not after an unexpected, powerful kiss that had brought back memories of a night when a sexy cowboy had corralled her into picking a number on the roulette wheel and had placed an impossibly large stack of chips on it.

She's still been in costume, having just finished a dance number and, as was custom, she and her fellow dancers strolled through the casino, chatting with guests and enticing them to stick around and part with their hard-earned money.

Tanya had hated that part of the job, mostly because

she ended up fighting off the roving hands of too many drunks, but Devlin had been a perfect gentleman.

Waiting outside the dressing room as she changed, taking her to an expensive dinner, insisting she join him and his entourage as his lucky charm after he'd won big on her choice of lucky thirteen.

It wasn't until hours later when they were alone in the elevator and on their way to his suite that he'd kissed her for the first time. Then he'd kissed her again and again as he'd laid her on the satin sheets of the king-size bed right before he—

"Tanya?" Dev's voice pulled her away from the memories. "What history? What are you talking about?"

Now wasn't the time and the men's locker room certainly wasn't the place, but she had a feeling Dev wouldn't let her put this off after she'd let the cat out of the bag.

She drew in another deep breath and decided to go with the Band-Aid removal method. All at once. "Reno, October 2003. Desert Kings Casino."

His brows dropped into a deep V over his eyes and she could tell he was trying to put the pieces together. "Yeah, I used to go there often. What about Reno?"

"Well, like you said, you were there, gambling, and doing quite well, I might add. I was a dancer in the nightly revue." She waved a hand down the front of her jacket. "Not wearing much more than I've got on now. Replace this with sequins and feathers and a pair of heels I used to be able to run a city block in…"

His eyes grew wide as recognition dawned. "That was you?"

She nodded. "So when you said over lunch on Monday that you thought we knew each other in another life, you were right. It was another life—for me, anyway."

"I remember that trip. Sort of." Dev rubbed the edge of one finger across the bridge of his nose, as if the action would help his memory. "Hell, that was back in my 'partying hard' days. I was there with a group of friends and I could've sworn I'd met a girl the last night of our stay. Her name was… It was…" He snapped his fingers. "Tannie!"

Surprised at how much it hurt to hear her old nickname on his lips, Tanya forced a smile. "Yes, that was the name I went by back then."

"But that was almost ten years ago." Sudden horror lit his expression. "You couldn't have been much older than—"

"I was twenty-one at the time."

The look of relief on his face was almost comical. "Wow, that's good to know. It's all coming back to me now. Dinner, dancing, winning big money." His eyes focused on her, the icy blue deepening as his voice softened. "The elevator, the hotel room, the bed…waking up alone the next morning."

She swallowed hard. "Yes, well, I thought that was for the best."

"So is that why you haven't told me all this before now? Because I didn't recognize you? Because it was just a night of wild, hot monkey sex to you?"

"No!" Tanya laid her hand over his mouth. "Shhh! There was no sex. Hot monkey or any other style. Look, can we finish this discussion at another time? Someplace a bit more private?"

Dev yanked her hand away. "What do you mean there was no sex? I remember holding you in my arms, kissing you, peeling off that little black dress with my teeth."

"Yes, there was all that." Her tone grew exasperated. "And then you promptly passed out on me while digging in your wallet for a condom!"

* * *

Twenty-four hours later, Devlin still felt like a schmuck.

To say that Tanya had shocked him yesterday morning would be putting it mildly.

He still couldn't get over the revelation that they'd shared an amazing night a decade ago.

A night he'd been too wasted to finish what he'd—what they'd—started.

He'd been a drunken fool.

Then he'd been another kind of fool yesterday as he'd just stood there while she'd raced from the changing room.

Not smart enough to follow her, he'd taken her advice and taken a nice, long shower, remaining beneath the pounding hot spray of water until one of the male staff had come into the locker room to check on him at Tanya's request. But by the time he was changed, she'd left the fitness center.

He glanced at the clock and shut down his current project. There was a meeting scheduled in his brother's office in a few minutes and there was no way he was missing it.

Liam had made himself scarce since they'd talked at the diner on Monday, and Bryant and Laurie hadn't arrived home from Chicago until late last night.

Pushing away from his desk, Dev grabbed the cane. He'd been sore this morning, but it was a good soreness. The kind that came from working out. He had Tanya and the bingo ladies to thank for that.

He also suspected he had Tanya to thank for getting at least six solid hours of sleep last night before the familiar searing pain reared to life again. What he would've given to have her and her magic fingers there beside him in his bed as he tried to relieve the leg cramp by himself.

Hell, he wanted her in his bed for reasons not related to her job talents at all.

Good thing he'd fired her yesterday.

Wanting to concentrate on this much-needed discussion with his brothers, Dev mentally set aside any thought of the acupuncturist/former showgirl and stopped by his first-floor bedroom suite to pick up a couple of things needed for this meeting.

Grabbing two bottles by their foil-covered necks with one hand, he made his way back across the great room in the huge log building that served as both his family's home and the headquarters for Murphy Mountain Log Homes.

An oversize stone fireplace surrounded by comfortable rustic leather furniture served as the reception area during business hours. The company's offices, conference rooms and a wide staircase that led to guest quarters on the second floor all branched out from here.

The private family area was in the wings that jutted from either side of the house with his parents in one and just him and Liam still living in the other wing. Ric, the only other single Murphy brother without kids, had left for the Air Force last fall and was now serving at a base in Italy.

He evaded the front desk where Katie still sat even though she'd been promoted from receptionist to executive assistant last fall, seeing how she basically took care of all the Murphy brothers' business dealings. Avoiding Nolan's office was easy, too, as his door was shut, a sign that the architect was hunched over his drafting table and didn't want to be disturbed.

Devlin couldn't guarantee that he'd respect Nolan's wishes.

He'd been pissed as hell to find out Liam and Bryant had taken up flying lessons, even more so that the family had made the decision not to tell him about it. And now he wanted some answers.

He walked into Liam's office, not surprised to find the company president behind his desk and on the phone. Bryant was sitting across from him, his nose buried in a financial report.

Devlin closed the door behind him with the tip of his cane and then sat the two bottles of champagne on Liam's desk with a loud thunk, glad to put them down.

His action caused both his brothers to finally look at him.

"Ah, my ten o'clock appointment just walked in," Liam said into the phone. "I'll call you back."

He hung up and both he and Bryant stared at the booze for a long moment before looking at Dev.

There was another empty chair, and the pain shooting across his lower back told him to sit, but Dev wanted the advantage of standing tall—while he still could—seeing how all of the Murphy brothers were close to six feet when on their feet.

"Well, hello there, Dev." Bryant finally spoke first as he folded his report in half, taking the time to crease the center before tucking it down next to him in the chair. "Isn't it a bit early for a cocktail?"

"Where in hell did you get those?" Liam asked.

"White's Liquors. Where else?"

Liam and Bryant shared a surprised look that their alcoholic brother had actually ventured into a liquor store. Yeah, Dev had made sure he was good and pissed about the reason why before he even got out of his Jeep.

As it was, he'd been in and out of the place in ten minutes.

"Why?" Liam pushed. "Why do you have those bottles with you?"

"Oh, these aren't mine. They're for you two. Don't we have some celebrating to do? Aren't you guys just a few flight lessons short of being full-fledged pilots?" Dev's words came out hard. "Please, don't tell me you kept your lessons a secret from everyone."

"You're pissed," Bryant said, leaning back in his chair.

Dev turned to stare at him. "Really? You figured that out all on your own? Good thing we let you handle all the money around here."

"What I don't get is why," Bryant continued. "We talked about this, about Liam being your backup for the helo this time last year when we first got the chopper. When you announced in the hospital you didn't plan on flying again—"

"Yeah, I thought the family decision had been *no one* was flying again," Dev interrupted. "That having a helicopter was a risk the business didn't want to continue to have on the books. But I guess I was wrong. Now we have a matching set of flyboys around here, don't we? The 'Flying Murphy Brothers.' Sounds like a damned circus act."

"Look, you made your decision not to fly again and we respect that." Liam leaned forward, his elbows perched on his desk. "Everyone knows the accident wasn't your fault and no one in this company, or this family, blames you for it. Your license has been reinstated. You want to pilot the new helo. Fine."

Dev heard the sincerity in his brother's words, but he didn't believe him. He couldn't. No matter what the official report had said about what happened that last day of July, the pilot was always responsible for his machine, both on the ground and in the air.

"Wait a minute." He'd finally caught up with what Liam had said. "Did you say new helo?"

Liam nodded. "We're in the process of purchasing a replacement helicopter for the business. That's what this is, Dev. A business decision. You know how much we came to depend on that piece of machinery in the few short months we had it."

"At what risk?" Devlin heard the door open behind him, but he didn't turn around, not caring who was standing there. "Is having that damn thing worth it? What if there's another crash? Those babies are expensive, you know. Just because one of the Murphy boys broke his toy doesn't mean we just run out and get another one."

Bryant pushed to his feet. "Hold on a minute, Dev—"

"What about your wife, Bry? Don't tell me Laurie is okay with the idea of you flying off into the wild blue yonder."

"Of course she's okay with this," Bryant snapped. "Look, no one is trying to clip your wings—"

"You want to know why I clipped my own wings?" Dev cut his brother off again, the fear and anger deep inside of him reaching a boiling point that was about to explode. "Because I'm scared! I'm damn scared of getting back in the air again. Scared of losing control while I have someone else up there with me."

"I'd fly with you again in a heartbeat."

Dev turned and found his eldest brother, Adam, standing there.

Adam, who'd served in the military for twenty years and had seen action in any number of far distant lands only to find his life in danger because his brother had crashed and burned last year, stranding them both for almost three days.

"I trust you with my life." Adam took a step closer. "I trust you with the lives of every single member of our family and if you ever need me to ride shotgun, I'm there."

"Me, too," Bryant added.

"Ditto," Liam chimed in.

"Are you all crazy?" Ignoring how his brothers' declarations made his heart swell, Dev barked out a sharp, humorless laugh, his gaze darting from one man to the next. "What if this happens again? What if we aren't so lucky next time? What if somebody winds up dead?"

Chapter Seven

Missing the days when the stomp of his boots echoed across the huge deck behind his family's home, Devlin settled for the quiet thud of canvas sneakers as he gingerly made his way down the steps and past the in-ground pool.

It was tough to stay pissed without the gratification of an old-fashioned boot stomping, but he'd been too unsteady on his feet this morning to pull on his handmade Tony Lamas.

Refusing to sit while he and his brothers had argued about fears, faults and replacing the helo meant his entire body was now in pain, from the headache threatening to split open his skull to the killer leg cramp just waiting to cripple him again.

Whether it was a physical reaction caused by his ongoing medical issues or from the burn of humiliation after admitting he was once again a loser, with a capital *L*, he didn't want to analyze it at the moment.

Adam trailed him, along with Adam's dog, Shadow, who had lived up to his name ever since he'd found the animal abandoned in a parking lot last summer.

Thankfully his brother remained silent, even if he stayed with him as Dev kept walking, concentrating on putting one foot in front of the other. The last thing he needed was to catch the tip of his cane in the flagstone crevices that surrounded the pool and have to be rescued.

Again.

He slowed a bit when the flagstone turned into a walkway that meandered past the gazebo, his mother's expansive flower beds and the log homes where Nolan and Bryant lived. Glancing at the almost finished cabin closest to the lake that would soon be Liam's place, he was surprised at how much work had been done already this spring. He'd never even noticed.

He'd been too damn busy thinking about himself.

Not ready to stop yet, he kept going until he passed the boathouse at the water's edge and stepped onto the wooden dock that stretched out twenty feet over the deep blue water of the lake. The walking was taking its toll on his already weak legs, but he refused to stop until he was damn good and ready.

"It's still a bit early in the season for a swim." Adam finally spoke. "But I've heard Mom say she's going to open the pool this weekend thanks to this unseasonably warm spring we've been having. Of course, the fact that the water can be heated to her preferred sauna level is another reason—"

"I don't need a babysitter, thanks just the same." Dev kept his gaze focused on the water. "Walking out of Liam's office was my way of ending a losing argument. You should've stayed with the winning team."

"We're all on the same team, Little D."

The childhood nickname, short for Little Devil, caused a sudden sting in Dev's eyes that he blinked away.

When Bryant, who was four years younger than him, had first been learning to speak, he'd had a hard time pronouncing Dev's name—it came out sounding like the word *devil* instead. Of course, his brothers picked up on it right away and the moniker stuck. Even his mother got in on the teasing, saying the title fit her middle son perfectly.

"Well, if you think I'm going to take a running leap off the end of the dock—even if I could—believe me, I'm not that far gone."

"You brought two bottles of booze into your boss's office."

Dev sighed and headed for the bench on the side of the boathouse. "I was trying to make a point."

Adam sat next to him and Shadow dropped to lie at his feet. "Yeah, we got that."

"I'm sure Liam has the champagne under lock and key by now."

"Why would he? We never locked up the booze from you before."

His brother had a point, but still…

Dev let his head drop back against the log wall, his gaze on the blue skies above. The morning sun felt good on his face and a deep breath brought in the earthy pungency of the land waking up and welcoming a new season.

"I was only an alcoholic before. Now, I'm a washed up pilot who crashed and burned within six months of getting his license. I can barely lift my arms over my head and if I go twenty-four hours without falling on my ass I consider it a good day."

Adam leaned forward, his head moving back and forth as he looked around.

"What are you doing?" Dev asked.

"Waiting for your pity party guests to arrive. I'm expecting a guy with a violin to appear any minute."

"Very funny, jerk."

They sat in silence for a few minutes before Adam spoke, his elbows on his knees, his gaze on the deck. "That accident was hell."

"Yeah, I know. I was there, remember?"

"It's okay to be scared. We all have our demons."

Dev looked at his brother knowing he was referring to something more than what they experienced last summer.

Post-traumatic stress had Adam seeking help from the local Veterans' Center after his return from Afghanistan, and he continued counseling for a while after the crash. He didn't go anymore, but the two of them had talked a few times while Dev had been hospitalized about the crash and the memories it had brought back to life.

"Yeah, I didn't do you any favors by dropping our asses in the forest, huh?"

"I never blamed you, Dev." Adam turned to him, his gaze strong. "I told you that when you finally came to that first day in the woods. Geez, I'm the one who came out with just a few scratches. And I'm doing much better. Mentally. Thanks to Fay and my little boy. The two of them are anchors I never knew I needed until they came into my life."

Dev tightened his grip on his cane and hefted it in the air. "I guess this is my anchor."

"For now, maybe. Not forever. You'll find what you're looking for."

Not sure how to answer that, Dev turned his attention to the lake and stayed silent, remembering all the amazing times he and his family had had growing up here.

From swimming to waterskiing to fishing, the Murphy place had always been the favorite hangout for the brothers and their friends. Even now, with two of his brothers married and a new generation of kids added to the mix, they still enjoyed both working and playing together.

Adam gave him an easy jab to the ribs, jolting Dev from his thoughts. "You know, when I mentioned taking a swim, I really was talking about the pool." He pointed back toward the yard. "Of course, Mom would be the only Wet Nana around…"

Dev groaned. He'd wondered last night how long it would take for the news to get around. "Who told you? Damn, that was only yesterday morning."

"Are you kidding? In a town this size? You joining the senior-citizen water exercise class is the talk of the beauty shop. Which our mother and Fay happened to be at yesterday afternoon."

"Great."

"There was talk about a very pretty and very young lady there with you—"

"Tanya's not that young." Now. But ten years ago in Reno, she'd only been twenty-one. "She's a few years behind me, that's all."

"Nice to know you've ended your self-imposed dating drought."

"Self-imposed? Seventy-five percent of my body was covered in plaster casts, mental splints and screws for the first six months after the crash. Makes it a little tough to grab dinner and movie, never mind an attempt at…"

Dev's voice trailed off as his thoughts jumped between his drunken ineptness ten years ago and his renewed sexual desire, absent after the crash until the moment he'd seen Tanya, and how the same woman was connected to both.

"At what?" Adam asked.

"At none of your damn business."

Adam grinned. "You've had plenty of nurses and lady friends ready to assist you and answer to your every… whim if you wanted."

Yeah, and he hadn't been interested in any of them.

So why now? Why Tanya? Was it because of the intimacy he'd felt between them from the moment he'd met her? A feeling he couldn't explain until she'd finally told him about the way their lives had intersected years earlier?

"Besides, we're not dating. Tanya is an acupuncturist and a massage therapist. She also does something with Chinese herbs, I think."

"You're working with an acupuncturist? 'No Needles, No Way' Devlin Murphy?"

The shock in Adam's tone made Dev laugh. "Yes. No. I don't know if we're working together or not. She's not sticking me with needles, but she does have some alternative ideas about assisting in my recovery."

"And you've got ideas about her."

His laughter faded. "I fired her yesterday."

"Why?" Adam's expression went from confusion to understanding. "*Because* you've got ideas about her," he repeated, "and paying her for services rendered while trying to render services of your own… Yeah, I can see where that would get messy."

"You don't know the half of messy."

Dev went on to tell his brother everything, from their chance meeting in Reno to her being Mac's granddaughter to Tanya's plans to be in London before the Fourth of July. He skipped over the part about the kiss in the men's locker room yesterday, but he could see Adam easily put the pieces together.

"Yeah, I appreciate your problem, bro," he said.

"Any advice?"

"Let her make you a pincushion and be done with it."

Dev shuddered at the thought of Tanya getting anywhere near him with those tiny, pointed... "You're not helping, man."

"Hey, like you helped me last summer? I was trying to make things right between me and Fay and you weren't exactly a fountain of wisdom."

"This is different. You were talking babies and engagement rings. I'd just like a second chance at—"

"At proving you're more than all talk and no action. Yeah, I get that." Adam checked his watch. "Look, I've got to head out. A.J. has a well-baby visit with the doctors."

"So you're just going to leave me hanging here?"

His brother's expression was one of faked sincerity. "Would I do that to you?"

"Hell, yeah, you would. And you'd enjoy every minute of it."

Adam laughed. "Okay, I'll give you the same advice you gave me. Back off. Let her come to you. Most of the women in this town, at least those between the ages of eight and eighty, eventually do."

"Very funny."

"All I'm saying is relax and stop overthinking everything." Adam got to his feet. "This is your first time back at the rodeo, so to speak. You as much as said you two already have something brewing, so let it brew. You've never had to chase a lady before. Why start now?"

Dev realized his brother had a point.

"Besides, if this one doesn't work out, another one will come along," Adam said over his shoulder as he headed back for the house. "They always do, don't they?"

Tanya shifted from one foot to the other, peeking down at her new wedge sandals—bright red gingham with cork heels and cute little bows. They perfectly matched the cotton fabric of her sundress, which was a bit dressier than her usual yoga wear. The shoes were also a bit flashy for her, but they were fun and a gift from her mom.

They also helped to distract her from the fact it'd been seven days since she'd seen or talked with Devlin.

Not counting voice mails or text messages.

She'd called last Thursday afternoon to check on him, feeling like a fool for rushing out of the men's locker room the day before.

Heck, she'd left like she was being chased by the devil.

Changing and scooting out of the fitness center instead of waiting for Dev seemed like the right thing to do at the time. She'd been worried he'd want to talk more about that kiss, or about what happened in Reno…or what hadn't happened.

Nothing like dropkicking a man's ego with one sentence.

Then again, she'd been humiliated, too, that long ago night, thinking she'd once again failed to keep a man's interest. Of course, later on she'd realized just how much he'd had to drink, but still… Not that any lingering hurt feelings had been the reason she'd blurted out—

Oh, darn! There went her good mood!

The line waiting to place orders at the front counter of Doucette's Bakery moved forward, so she took a step to keep her place then gave in and checked her phone again.

No new calls. No new messages.

Dev had finally responded to the voice mail she'd left him last week with a brusque text.

Feel fine.

Gee, why hadn't she been surprised by that response? Fine had to be the man's favorite word.

So she had planned to wait until Friday morning before reaching out again, purely on a professional basis of course, but then Mac had surprised her by suggesting a weekend trip to Colorado Springs in his vintage biplane to visit with her family.

She's placed another call to Devlin that same Thursday afternoon, and received another text message by nine o'clock that night.

Have a good time. See you when you get back.

No exclamation points, no smiley faces, no enthusiasm of any type.

It was now Wednesday afternoon. She'd been back in Destiny since Monday evening and she still hadn't seen him, despite another voice mail when she'd got back to town.

They were supposed to be working together, weren't they?

Maybe after everything that happened last week—not to mention ten years ago—Dev had been serious when he fired her.

She still thought aquatic therapy was a good supplement to his rehabilitation treatment, when Dev bothered to go. Maybe she should give his therapist a call and suggest—

"Excuse me, miss, can I take your order?"

She jumped at the words and shuffled forward, realizing she was next. "Sorry about that."

Pushing any thoughts of Dev from her mind, she placed her order and minutes later walked out into the late afternoon sunshine with her dinner in a paper bag decorated with the deli's dragonfly logo.

It was another warm day, and with Mac working late at the airstrip she didn't want to drive back to the cabin and eat alone. The white gazebo in the town square, surrounded by already budding cottonwood trees, would be a perfect place for an impromptu picnic. She decided to leave her car in the parking lot behind the deli and head for the wooden structure.

Walking down the street, Tanya spotted Sherry's Diner across the way and remembered how Dev's brother Liam had offered a tour of the family business when she'd met him there.

Hmm, maybe she'd give Dev one more day.

If he didn't get in touch with her by tomorrow, she'd drive over to the Murphy Mountain Log Homes head-quarters after Mac's acupuncture session in the morning.

There was nothing wrong with being proactive. If he'd been serious when he decided he didn't want her work-ing with him, no matter what the reason, he was going to have to tell in her person.

Waiting for a break in the traffic, she skipped across the street to the center square. The scent of fresh-cut grass surrounded her, mixing with the heady aroma of the flow-ers blooming around each of the trees.

She smiled as she headed down the sidewalk, but the sight of Dev sitting on the steps of the gazebo had her skid-ding to a stop, almost tripping over her pretty new shoes.

He was dressed casually in jeans, a button-down shirt with the sleeves rolled back and those now-familiar cow-boy boots. A felt Stetson perched on his head completed the stereotypical but oh, so sexy look of a true Wyoming cowboy.

Unable to move, she stood there and watched as he un-wrapped the sandwich in his lap from the familiar brown paper of Doucette's Bakery. He then raised the stuffed roll to his mouth and lazily looked out over the expanse of lawn before his eyes locked onto her feet.

Tanya resisted the silly urge to wiggle her toes as he took his time running his gaze up over her simple sun-dress until she reached her face.

He dropped his sandwich to his lap, touched the brim of his Stetson lightly and smiled. "Well, hello there."

Geez, his in-person attitude was nothing like those pitiful texts he'd left. Three words and she was blushing? She quickly blamed her reaction on his smile and the memories of being in his arms that were suddenly running through her head like a movie projector.

"Hi, yourself." Happy at how casual her greeting sounded, she held the deli bag aloft. "Great minds think alike."

"Looks that way." He waved at the empty spot next to him. "There's plenty of room. Come have a seat."

Not bothering to debate if she should or not, Tanya joined him, careful as she stepped over his outstretched leg. "Thanks."

Tucking her skirt beneath her, she sat and pulled in a quick breath, hoping it would calm her racing heart, but all it did was surround her with his now-familiar warm, musky scent. She busied herself with laying out her sandwich, the small container of macaroni salad and the icy-cold bottle of lemonade.

Ignoring her shaky fingers would've been easier if Dev hadn't reached over and captured them in his, along with the wobbly napkin that had been a dead giveaway to her nervousness.

"It doesn't have to be this awkward."

She pulled in another deep breath, released it and looked up at him. "It feels pretty awkward. Especially after those texts you sent."

This time it was Dev's turn to blush, and darn if the ruddy color across his cheeks didn't make the man even more handsome. "Yeah, I'm sorry about that. Last Thursday was a tough day for a lot of reasons."

Curious, but not wanting to push, Tanya only said, "Apology accepted."

"That was easy." Dev grinned. "Here I thought I might have to work a bit harder to get back into your good graces. Like, maybe kissing you again—"

"No!"

He let go when she pulled back, his smile even wider now. "You don't have to answer with such conviction."

"I'm sorry, that didn't come out… That's not what I meant."

He leaned in close. "So you do want me to kiss you again?"

Focusing on her sandwich, she matched his hushed tone. "This isn't the time or place for that."

"You let me know when it is the right time and place."

Her gaze shot up to his as he straightened. His roguish smile should have made her nervous, considering her recent romantic history. Heck, she should be running for the hills, but all she could think about was how much she wanted a kiss from him for a third time.

And then a fourth time.

A fifth time.

She shifted her legs to use her lap for a makeshift table and found her bare knees brushing against his jean-clad thigh. A sizzle danced over her skin, but Dev didn't seem to notice, his attention back on his own sandwich.

Would there be a right time and place?

Not for kissing. No, there couldn't be any more of that, but they probably should talk about what happened last week, especially if they were going to work together.

Were they still going to work together?

Tanya had no idea.

She wanted to—a surprise considering how much she'd been against the idea only two weeks ago. Maybe deep

down she'd known something like what had happened
between them in the locker room would come to pass.

Maybe she'd wanted that kiss to happen.

No! That had been a fluke, but she was sure she could
help Dev if he'd only let her—

"So, what's in that thing? It looks a bit too green for
me." Dev gestured at her sandwich before taking a bite
of his own.

Tanya blinked, pulled from her thoughts by his question. She looked down at her food and tried to recall what
she'd asked for.

"Uh, mozzarella, tomatoes, sliced cucumbers, avocado,
shredded lettuce and alfalfa sprouts on a whole-wheat roll.
I had to order it special."

"I'm not surprised."

"I didn't see you in the deli," she said, pushing the es-
caping sprouts back between the edges of bread. "How
did you get your meal?"

"My niece," he mumbled around a mouthful, then swallowed. "Abby works at the bakery. I rode shotgun while
she drove my Jeep around for a while this afternoon. She's
working on getting her driver's license. In return I got
car-side delivery. I was going to head back to my office,
but I've been chained to my desk all week so I decided to
relax and enjoy the sunshine."

As much as she wanted to talk about what happened
last week, Dev seemed intent on just keeping things light
and easy. "So what's in your sandwich?" she asked instead.

"What isn't? It's the Doucette Deli Special. Roast beef,
turkey, ham, salami, provolone, lettuce, tomato, pickles
and a spicy kind of mayo."

"How can you eat all that?" She leaned over and held
her sandwich next to his. "Look, it's twice the size of
mine."

"What can I say?" Dev grinned. "I've got a big appetite."

A flirty retort sprang to her lips, but Tanya held back and concentrated instead on her meal. A quick peek through her lashes told her Dev was doing the same, and they sat in a friendly silence for a few minutes, enjoying their food.

Dev waved and returned greetings to people who called out to him, several of whom were female. Everyone made a comment about how nice it was to see him up and around again.

"Does that bother you?" she asked.

He lifted one shoulder in a casual shrug that seemed to freeze in place for a moment before he slowly lowered it. "People are just being nice. So how was your trip home?"

"Oh, it was great." She smiled, remembering a time when she hadn't been able to say that about being with her family. "And flying there in Mac's plane was amazing! The open cockpit made me feel like a bird! You must miss it so much."

He adjusted the brim of his Stetson, pulling it lower over his brow before he wrapped up the remains of his sandwich and shoved it back into the paper bag. "Yeah, it's a real kick being up there."

"I'll admit I was scared at first," Tanya gushed. "But the moment the wheels left the ground… Oh, the feeling of freedom! We had to delay our return until Monday afternoon due to weather, but arriving at sunset just took my breath away."

"It'll do that."

Dev shifted, one hand pressed hard against the wood surface and she realized for the first time that sitting here this long wasn't doing his back or leg any favors.

"Are you okay?" she asked. "No, you're not. I should've realized—"

"I'm fine."

She fought the urge to roll her eyes. There was that word again. "Dev, we can finish this—"

"I said, I'm fine." His words were abrupt, but then he smiled again and asked, "Did you do anything special during your visit?"

Surprised at his insistence and instinctively knowing he wasn't feeling as well as he claimed, she relented for the moment. "I went shopping with my mom for prom dresses."

Dev offered a raised eyebrow. "Prom dresses?"

"For my sisters. My half-sisters, actually. Carly and Alexis are twins. Mom remarried during my freshman year in high school and they were born a year later, a week after my fifteenth birthday."

Dev reached for his iced tea, speaking around the straw. "That must've made life interesting."

"Actually, I was a bit of troublemaker long before the babies arrived. My mom was busy dating Paul, then planning a wedding and whoops, three months later she was pregnant."

Tanya was glad she could look back on that time in her life, realize what a mess she'd been and how lucky she was to come out on the other side in one piece, even if the old twinges still appeared every now and then. "The babies were a big distraction and I used that as an excuse to... Well, let's just say I was on my own by the time I was seventeen. Married and dancing in Reno two years later."

"M-married?" Dev sputtered.

"The marriage lasted less than a year," Tanya quickly added. "My ex was more interested in gambling and other pursuits than in me. I was single when you and I...met."

Dev shifted again, and this time a frown crossed his features.

"Look, whether you want to admit it or not, I can tell you're hurting," she pushed. "You don't have to wait for me. You can go—"

"Tanya, I'm not going anywhere." Dev reached over and took her hand again. "I'm guessing from your reaction last week you don't go by Tannie anymore."

She shook her head, sending her ponytail flying. "No, it's Tanya now."

"Okay." He gave her fingers a gentle squeeze. "Look, the past couple of days have been crazy busy. This is the first chance I've had to take a breath, but that's just an excuse. I should've called once you let me know you were back in town."

"Yeah, I was wondering about that." She folded her hand into his, surprised at how natural the move was. "I guess we can't avoid talking about…everything. Do you want to go somewhere more private? Like back to the cabin?"

Dev closed his eyes. "I don't know if that's a good idea."

"Dev—"

"Hey, I'm being honest. Being alone out here in public is a lot different than being—"

"Oh, honey!" A sweet voice called out. "There you are!"

Tanya and Dev turned at the same time, dropping their hold on each other.

Conscious of the tingling in her palm, she brushed her hand lightly across her skirt as a petite woman dressed in capri slacks and a pretty top, her gray hair worn in a stylish bob, hurried up the sidewalk toward them.

Dev groaned softly. "Hello, Mother."

"Devlin, we have an emergency and need your help right away."

"Is it Dad?" He shot to his feet and Tanya automatically reached out to steady him, but he only swayed for a moment before finding his center. "Someone at the house?"

His mother dismissed his questions with a wave of her hand. "Oh, I didn't mean to scare you. No, it's not a family matter. Well, at least not our family, but Burt, the fireman who's been calling the weekly bingo games since your accident, is sick with the flu."

He visibly relaxed, bracing one hand on the closest column. "That's your big emergency?"

"We need you, Dev. The firehouse needs you. Now get your butt over to the church hall. Pronto."

Chapter Eight

Dev fought against the twinges of red-hot pain snaking across his shoulders and lower back, thankful he'd been able to get to his feet and stay there. He let go of the column he'd used to catch himself and moved down off the bottom step of the gazebo to the pavement.

Switching out of his sneakers earlier had probably been the wrong decision, especially since he'd had a physical therapy session this morning, but he felt more like himself wearing his boots.

Besides, he hadn't planned on doing much walking.

Or making sudden moves.

He crossed his arms over his chest and stared at his mother. He loved the woman more than his own life, but seriously?

Bingo?

Running into Tanya unexpectedly had him putting Adam's advice into action. He'd tried to keep the conversation casual, but just a few moments ago they'd started to talk about something more important than sandwiches, flying and prom dresses.

Although finding out she'd been married as a teenager had surprised the hell out of him.

Still, he wanted to see where their conversation might lead, especially since she'd hinted they should talk about Reno. The memories were still few and far between, but there was one thing he wanted to say to her.

"Honey, are you okay?" his mother asked. "You look a bit pale."

"I'm fine, Mom." Boy, the last thing he needed right now was interference from a woman who had meddling down to an art form. "And you know I'm not calling the weekly bingo night anymore. I haven't since the crash last year."

"I'm well aware of that, but tonight you're getting back in the game. So to speak." Elise Murphy's proud posture made her seem much taller than her five-foot frame. It was a familiar stance that told Dev arguing was useless. "They need someone who's familiar with the rules and the equipment."

"Burt doesn't have a backup?"

"Timmy Ouellette's wife is in labor and he's with her at the hospital. So that leaves you."

Still Dev hesitated. He hadn't been to the firehouse since he'd started coming back to town. Other than running into a few of his former coworkers last week, he hadn't talked with anyone else from the department.

Of course, the town's weekly bingo game was held in the church hall, not the actual firehouse, but it still meant being surrounded by whichever crew members weren't on call, including the fire chief.

A man Devlin admired and had yet to have one of the

hardest conversations of his life with. And that included the time he'd admitted to his family he was an alcoholic.

"Bingo sounds like fun."

Dev turned. Tanya had gotten to her feet and now stood next to him. His gaze caught and held on her painted toes—a bright blue this time—peeking out of the ends of those sexy shoes of hers. He just knew images of her wearing them, and nothing else, were going to invade his dreams tonight.

His mother cleared her throat, bringing Dev back to reality. "Oh. Mom, this is Tanya Reeves. Tanya, this is my mother, Elise Murphy."

"Why, hello! You're Steven Mackenzie's granddaughter, right? It's so nice to have you back in town again!" His mother relaxed her stance and offered Tanya a bright smile. "I've wanted to meet the woman who's helping my son. I'm told you're an acupuncturist. You do know he's deathly afraid of needles, right?"

Tanya glanced at him for a moment before turning her attention to the whirlwind that was his mother. "Ah, yes, I'm aware of his aversion. It's nice to meet you, too."

"But you did get him into the water, which I think is terrific." Elise laid a hand on Tanya's arm. "You know, I've thought about joining the Wet Nanas, seeing how I'm a grandmother, too. I was under the impression the workouts weren't that strenuous, but if it's good enough for a strong man like my son, I think I might have to give the group a second look."

Dev leaned in close to Tanya, the brim of his Stetson brushing against her hair, and said in a staged whisper, "I'm never going back to that class again."

"I heard that." Elise let go and frowned at him.

"You were meant to."

He tried to ignore how Tanya's body had shivered when

he'd whispered into her ear and smiled at his mom to take the sting from his words. Keeping his grin in place even though he knew it wouldn't do him any good, Dev continued, "And I know there are at least two or three members of the fire department who can pull a ball and call the number. Hey, what about—"

"No one has your charm or wit, so please stop trying to get out of this and accept your civic duty." His mother cut him off, her attention now on her purse as she rooted around inside the oversize bag. "You can bring Tanya along as your date, of course."

Dev opened his mouth to protest yet again, but decided the best defense was to give in.

He looked over at Tanya, wondering if this form of small-town entertainment was something she'd be interested in. "Would you like to come tonight? Not as a date, but as a…friend?"

"I don't know." She gave him an uncertain smile. "I haven't played bingo since I was a kid—"

"Oh, then you must join us," Elise interrupted her. "The games can be fast and furious, but I won't let you get lost. There are all sorts of prizes, from gift baskets to cash. You can sit with me and my crowd."

"Yeah, you'll be my mother's date."

His mother swatted him, but continued talking, "Fay and Laurie will be there, too, and I'll even let you borrow one of my daubers. It'll be fun!"

Confusion filled Tanya's pretty eyes as she glanced between his mother and him. "A dauber? Ah, okay."

"It's a plastic bottle of liquid ink with a sponge tip that's used to mark the paper game cards," Dev explained, suddenly not so sure that Tanya hanging around his mother and sisters-in-law was such a good idea. Not that he could do anything about it now. "Mom's got one in every color of the rainbow. She's very particular about using certain colors for certain games."

"But I have extras in blue, pink, yellow and red, so you can have your pick." Elise glanced down at Tanya's shoes. "I think blue and red are your colors. And I just love those shoes, very chic."

"Thanks." Tanya's smile brightened as she peeked down at her shoes. "They are kind of sassy, aren't they?"

Yep, they'd definitely be in his dreams tonight.

His mother swiped her thumb over the cell phone she'd retrieved from her bag. "Oh, it's almost six o'clock. You two better head to the church hall. The doors are just about to open even though the first game isn't for another thirty minutes. Plenty of time for you to give Tanya a few helpful hints on the game, honey."

Dev watched his mother work her phone's keyboard with the proficiency of a teenager. Unlike him. He hated the small buttons, which was why his replies to Tanya last week had been short and sweet.

Okay, not so sweet.

And his lack of typing skills wasn't the only reason.

He'd decided to put some distance between them—just like his brother had suggested—and her out-of-town weekend trip had fit perfectly into his plan.

When she hadn't contacted him on Monday morning, he'd gone about his day as usual. He'd planned to get in touch with her the next morning, but he hadn't been kidding about things being crazy around the office. He'd been stuck in meetings for the past two days and this afternoon had been his first time out of the office except for two trips down to Laramie for his physical therapy.

He'd been considering texting her after he'd finished eating, but before he could, lo and behold, there she was, standing right in front of him. Once she'd joined him, he'd tossed his plan to back off out the window, especially when he found himself offering to kiss her again.

"Oh, shoot, that's over the limit." Elise Murphy frowned and went back to her typing.

"What are you doing?" Dev asked.

"I'm tweeting the news about you being the bingo caller tonight, of course!" His mother grabbed his arm and gave a tug. Dev instinctively bent at the waist so she could give him a kiss on the cheek. "I'll see both of you soon!"

"B-13!"

Dev looked out over the crowd of bent heads and busy hands. He waited, wanting to give everyone a chance to match the number to their game cards, but still no winner.

Cover-All was one of the longest bingo games because the winner had to fill every square on their card, and most players were working, on average, six cards, but it'd been over an hour since the last break and Dev was ready for one.

In the past, he'd done this job entirely on his feet, but not tonight. His leg was killing him, not to mention the stiffness that had settled in his shoulders, and the wooden stool behind the table only gave him a modicum of relief.

"Come on, people, we must have a winner out there somewhere. Who wants this beautiful, handmade quilt as a prize?" He placed the ball in its designated cubbyhole and the corresponding number lit up on the board behind him.

"The quilt's not even full size." The retort came from somewhere in the back, but Dev recognized the craggy female voice. "What's a person to do with it, anyway?"

"Oh, I don't know, Mrs. Honeyfield." *Geez, what a name for one of most crotchety women in town.* Dev kept his tone light and teasing, having noticed the outraged expression on one of the older ladies down front who'd probably created the prize with her own hands. "I can picture cuddling beneath this beauty in front of a fire on a cold winter's night. Or perhaps taking it on a picnic up in the mountains?"

"Sounds great! Are you part of the prize, too?"

This came from one of the female firefighters working the nearby concession stand and Dev laughed along with the rest of the crowd.

For many, the weekly bingo night was the highlight of their social calendar and his job as caller had always been one part master of ceremonies, one part entertainer and one part time manager.

He'd forgotten how much he enjoyed the back-and-forth banter that went along with raising money for many worthwhile causes in Destiny. It also surprised him how easily everything had come back to him.

He'd confided in Tanya he'd been nervous as they walked here after stopping by his Jeep to retrieve his cane. She'd asked about his pain level again, but he'd assured her that walking helped. Their arrival at the hall caused quite a stir and Dev had soon found himself surrounded by old friends, well-wishers and, of course, his fellow firefighters.

A few minutes later his mother had showed up and whisked Tanya away with a promise to walk her though the fundamentals of the game. They sat at a long table on the far right-hand side of the room and Dev's gaze strayed toward them often.

And he couldn't stop himself from looking at her again right now. Tanya seemed to be having a good time, talking and laughing with the group of ladies sitting there, three of whom were his family.

And a newcomer that definitely wasn't.

In fact, the tall, hulking wall of muscle was decidedly male.

Dev watched as the man pulled out the empty seat next to Tanya and sat, holding out his hand to introduce himself.

A burning sensation raced through Dev's body again, but this time it had nothing to do with his injuries. It was jealousy, pure and simple, an emotion he couldn't remember feeling in a long time, especially where a woman was concerned.

Had he been jealous when the Red Sox had crushed his beloved Rockies in the '07 World Series? Hell, yeah. When his eldest brother had spent a year studying in Paris? Sure. A bit green eyed whenever he saw someone enjoying a beer on a hot summer day? That was something he was still learning to live with, even after six years of sobriety, but he'd never felt envious over a woman before.

Why would he when there were so many out there to choose from?

"What's the matter, Murphy?" The guy next to Tanya sat back in his seat, stretching his arm across the back of her chair, his voice rising above the din. "You're thinking a bit too long about that offer."

Catcalls and whistles pulled Dev from his thoughts, reminding him of the unanswered question about being part of the game's prize. "We'll see what can be arranged," he finally said, his good mood taking a quick turn downward.

He tightened his fingers around the microphone and grabbed another numbered ball. "G-48!"

It was another six numbers before someone finally shouted "Bingo!"

Dev looked up and found Adam's wife on her feet, waving a game card over her head. It was about time. "Looks like we have a winner, folks."

"Hey! No fair! She's already got herself one of the Murphy boys!"

More laughter from the room.

"Okay, we'll check Fay's winning card during this next break," Dev said to the crowd as his sister-in-law made her way toward him. "You've got thirty minutes to refresh your drinks or grab a bowl of blue-ribbon, five-alarm chili from the best firehouse cooks in the state."

The noise level grew as people rose to stretch their legs and visit the restrooms and each other. Dev turned off the microphone and dropped into the nearest folding chair. It wasn't the most comfortable seat, but it was better than that damn stool.

"You're looking a little tired." Fay handed off her winning game card to the pastor, who was acting as official verifier for tonight's winners. "Your mom is worried about you."

"This was her idea, you know." He reached for his water bottle and took a long swallow. "I could be home right now watching a ball game with the guys."

"Or you could be spending time with your nice Ms. Reeves."

It took some effort, but Dev kept his gaze from going across the room again. "Tanya's not *my* Ms. Anything."

"This is so pretty. The pastel colors aren't quite right for A.J.'s room, but maybe…" Fay's words trailed off as she traced the pattern on the quilt. "She's not? Oh, I must've misunderstood. Well, I'm sure Dean will appreciate knowing that Tanya's not yours." She turned to look at him. "Did you notice he stopped by during this last game?"

Yeah, he'd noticed, and that was before Dean had opened his mouth with his wisecrack.

It was kind of hard to miss Dean Zippenella. The guy stood over six feet tall and could bench-press a Volkswagen Beetle if he wanted to. He'd moved to Destiny a couple of years ago when his best friend, Bobby Winslow, had returned.

"Of course, your mom pointed out how much Dean and Tanya have in common," Fay continued, "considering their career fields."

That made sense. Dean was a physical therapist at the Veterans' Center down in Laramie, and while either one of them could assist with his aching muscles, Dev preferred to have Tanya's magic hands on his body right now.

"Mom also told Tanya she absolutely has to see Dean's master bedroom."

Dev choked on the last of his water. Wiping at his mouth with the back of his hand, he didn't miss the mischief in Fay's eyes. "What the hell does that mean?"

"That wall of glass that looks out over the mountains? Your mom is so proud of Nolan's design work on that place. I've got to admit it's pretty impressive."

"When have you ever been in Zip's bedroom?" Dev tried to keep his tone light, even though the idea of Tanya being anywhere near Zip, or his log home, burned as hot as the pain dancing down his leg. "And where was Adam at the time?"

"My husband was right there with me and it was during the final inspection of the house," Fay said, and then smiled. "Of course, that was before it was furnished. Zip says he's got a king-size bed with a ton of pillows. Which makes sense, I mean, the guy is so big—"

"Okay, that's enough." Dev cut off his sister-in-law. "The last thing I want to hear about is some guy's… furniture."

"Does that mean I shouldn't mention that your mother also said—"

The pastor joined them and Fay stopped midsentence.

She accepted the quilt, hugging it to her chest as the two of them chatted for a few minutes about the blessing ceremony Fay and Adam were planning for A.J. in a few weeks.

Dev waited until he and Fay were alone again, and then said, "I know I'll regret asking, but what else did Mom say?"

"Oh, she just made it clear that Tanya was already spoken for."

Spoken for? What century was this?

He opened his mouth, but for once had no idea how to respond, other than to snap his jaw shut and roll his eyes.

"You know your mom, Dev." Fay poked a finger into his shoulder. "Playing matchmaker is one of her favorite hobbies. She told us how cozy you and Tanya looked eating dinner in the gazebo, which I thought was very sweet. Of course, Tanya was a bit—"

"Devlin Murphy? Sweet?" A low, rumbling voice that sounded like cars driving over gravel cut through the din of the crowd. "Now there's two things I'm not sure I'd ever put together."

Dev got to his feet so fast his body didn't have time to register how utterly wrong the sudden movement would be.

Everything went numb from his waist down, and he had no idea how he was still on his feet. Thankfully, the table was close enough for him to grab on to it, but his cane was out of reach.

"Ch-chief." Dev fought to keep his voice steady as he faced the man who led the town's fire department. "It's good to see you again."

Dressed in his typical uniform of black pants, white short-sleeved shirt with the DFD shoulder patch on his left arm and the gold five-crossed bugle collar pins that showed his rank, Chief Alex Morgan had been with the fire department as long as Dev had been alive.

"Good to see you, too, Murphy," he said, his upper lip barely visible beneath the groomed but bushy handlebar mustache Dev had never seen the man without. "Especially since the last time we talked you were flat on your back in a hospital bed."

And he was probably minutes away from being flat on his back again, right here in the church hall. "Yes, I remember."

"Well, I'll let you men talk while I head back." Fay scooted around the back of the table and rose up on her toes to place a quick kiss on Dev's cheek.

He then felt the cool rubber grip of his cane being pressed into his hand.

He offered his sister-in-law a look of thanks as he wrapped his fingers around the handle, taking a moment to steady himself while the chief was distracted by a couple of teenagers asking about the fire department's cadet program for high school juniors and seniors.

"Get them while they're young, huh?" Dev asked, surer of his ability to remain upright as sensation returned to his legs. He'd rather have the pain than nothing at all. "I should've started that way."

"You came to us when it was the right time for you."

The man was right. If Dev had joined the department's volunteer squad after he'd moved back home following college, his drinking would've gotten him kicked out within the first year.

Either that or killed.

Now it was time for Dev to do his own butt kicking. He'd been asked by his fellow—or should he say former—coworkers earlier in the evening about his recovery and when he was coming back to the department. Their questions had been heartfelt, but all Dev could think about was how he was no longer one of them.

Now was the moment to face that reality head on.

"Chief, this probably isn't the right time or place, but if you have a few minutes…"

The man nodded and pointed at a couple of chairs against the back wall, next to the lighted display of called numbers. "How about we head over there?"

Dev nodded, thankful he could manage to walk the short distance. But when he got there, he ignored the folding chair.

Determined to do this standing up, he compromised by at least bracing his back against the wall. "I'll be dropping by your office soon with an official notice in writing, but I want to let you know I'm resigning from the department's volunteer ranks."

"Denied."

Dev blinked, sure he hadn't heard the man correctly. "Excuse me?"

"You heard me. Your resignation is denied. You're not going anywhere."

"Chief, anyone can tell just from looking at me I can't fulfill the duties of a firefighter." Dev lowered his voice; he was gripping his cane with both hands now. "I'm no good to the department anymore."

"You having a HUYA moment?" Chief shoved his hands in his pocket.

Dev sighed. The chief's acronym, a favorite of his, stood for an event that happened often around the firehouse. Officially known as a Head Up Your A—

"You done now?" He didn't wait for Dev to answer. "Good. Did any of the crew mention the upcoming firefighters' competition?"

They had, and Dev had only nodded politely during

any talk about the annual event firefighters from various towns participated in. The weekend-long competition, being held in nearby Johnson City this year, consisted of a variety of challenges, both team and individual, designed to test the skill and abilities of the firefighter and provide entertainment to both the teams and the public who attended.

He'd been last year's overall winner after competing with Destiny's team ever since he'd joined the department five years ago.

"We've got six weeks to get ready and there are a couple of rookies on the team who could use some expert help." Someone called the chief's name. He motioned that he heard, but kept on talking. "Stop by my office and pick up the training schedule."

He couldn't believe what he was hearing. "Chief, I can't—"

"Is it your day job? I'm sure you're still trying to get caught up, but that never got in the way of your volunteer work before."

Dev shook his head. The chief misunderstood. "It's not a matter of time. Look at me. I have nothing to contribute—"

"You have a brain, a mouth and experience. Your department and fellow firefighters need you, son. Don't let us down."

With that, the man walked away, and Dev felt helpless to do anything but watch him go.

What in the hell was he going to do now?

The pastor waved at him and then pointed to his watch, a silent message that the break was just about over.

Except Dev decided the night was over for him.

Now, how to get out of—

An idea popped into his head that would solve at least

a few of his problems. He made it back to the head table as the crowd returned to their seats.

"Ladies and gentlemen, we have a special surprise for you all." Dev paused, waiting for the noise to die down. He pressed the cane close to his side, doing his best to keep it out of sight as he addressed the crowd. "Tonight's last hour of games will be led by a guest caller. Now, this is someone who's been a terrific fill-in for me a few times in the past, so I'm sure he won't mind helping out again tonight. Dean Zippenella. Come on down, Zip!"

Dev watched as first surprise and then a knowing grin crossed Dean's face. He got to his feet, acknowledging the crowd's applause with a wave of his hand before leaning over and whispering something to Tanya.

The sight of his friend's head so close to hers was the icing on an already bitter cake, and the way she smiled at whatever the man said didn't help. Then again, nothing at the moment was going to improve his mood.

When Zip finally joined him, Dev muted the microphone, handed it off and then shared a quick handshake with the man. "They're all yours," he said. "Enjoy."

"This wasn't necessary, you know." Zip shot back. "Your 'hands off' glare came through loud and clear."

"No idea what you're talking about, man."

Zip only grinned, turned the microphone back on and addressed the crowd. "How about a big round of applause for Devlin Murphy? We've missed having him here and let's hope we can get him back to the weekly bingo nights on a regular basis real soon."

Now it was Dev's turn to wave to the crowd as he grabbed his Stetson from the end of the table. Picking speed over grace, he walked away as quickly as he could while Zip got the evening started back up with a new game.

Dev reached the concession area, tucked into the corner

of the room near one of the exits. Waving off any offers of food, he quickly donned his hat and asked for a soda, enjoying the feel of the icy-cold can when handed to him.

Damn, this would be great rolled across his lower back.

He set the can down and tried to open it one-handed, unwilling to let go of his cane. Failing that, he glanced around for the closest chair, knowing he had to sit down, but then graceful fingers appeared and quickly popped the top for him.

He didn't have to turn to know Tanya had left her bingo cards to join him; her familiar scent, a mixture of sharp lemon citrus and sweet lavender, surrounded him. He'd been intrigued by that scent earlier tonight at the gazebo, and it clung to his clothes, wafting up to his nose every time he'd moved tonight.

"Can I do anything to help?" she asked.

"You just did." He took a long swallow, enjoying the cold liquid as it rushed down his throat.

"I can tell you're hurting." Her soft voice filled his ear. "Is it your leg again?"

"As a matter of fact, it is," Dev snapped, glaring at her. "What do you suggest we do about it? Drop my jeans right here so your magic fingers can go to work again?"

"Actually, I had something else in mind." She lifted the can from his grip and set it down on the table. "Now, give me your hand."

Chapter Nine

"Excuse me?"

Tanya ignored Dev's expression and reached for the hand that didn't have a death grip on the cane. Ignoring the now-familiar tingling sensation as her fingers brushed his, she slid her hand against his palm. Using her thumb, she quickly found the fleshy area on the back of his hand between his thumb and forefinger.

"What are you doing?" Dev demanded.

"Just give me a moment." Pressing firmly and evenly, Tanya manipulated the pressure point with ease. "This isn't going to produce the same results as needles—um, as an acupuncture session—but you should start to feel some relief in only a few minutes."

"That's cra...zy."

She offered him a raised eyebrow as his voice trailed off, knowing the acupressure was already working.

While she'd enjoyed the evening's fun, watching the

rising pain in Dev as he moved around, even though he'd done his best to hide the effects, had torn at her heart.

Meeting Dev's sisters-in-law, Fay and Laurie, had been nice, too, even if they, along with Dev's mother and her friends, had been way too interested in her connection to him.

She'd tried to make it clear that their interactions were strictly business and that it'd been her grandfather's idea, but she'd seen the glances and knowing smiles exchanged among the women.

Playing bingo alongside everyone else, she watched Dev's easy rapport with the crowd and how he really seemed to be having a good time. Right up until the last game. That's when she guessed the discomfort had gotten too much to bear.

When he'd headed to the concession stand she'd seen his ungainly walk and nothing could have kept her from going to him.

"Hey, that's not bad."

The surprise on Dev's face made her smile. "I'm certain whatever pain you're feeling isn't completely gone, but lessened maybe?"

"Enough so that I won't fall flat on my face any time soon."

"It's called acupressure. I did the same thing to help get rid of your leg cramp last week, remember?"

He curled his fingers around her hand, lightly caressing her knuckles. "Yeah, I remember."

Darn those sparks! "The relief won't last long," she said, pulling from his touch, "but you should be okay until you can get off your feet."

"Thanks. Sorry to take you away from your fun."

"I've had enough fun." A step backwards created much-needed space between them that allowed the cool breeze coming from the open doorway to brush against her body. "I told your mom she could finish playing my cards."

"You're leaving?"

"Aren't you?"

Dev nodded, looking at his hand as he flexed it a few times. "Yeah, I'm done for the night. Besides, it looks like Zip's got a handle on things. As usual."

Tanya glanced over at the big man, who was busy calling numbers and playing to the crowd with the same ease as Dev. "Yes, he seems to be having a good time."

She'd been surprised when the good-looking man with biceps that tested the seams of his short-sleeved T-shirt sat down beside her and started flirting.

And not just with her. He'd put his dazzling smile and sexy brown eyes to good use with all the ladies—young and old—sitting at the table.

Then Devlin's mother and sisters-in-law, in whispered tones so as not to disturb the game, had talked about her and Dean's related occupations and the beauty of his log home.

But when the man had offered a personal tour of his place if anyone was interested, Elise Murphy had actually told him to take his wanton ways elsewhere as everyone at the table was taken.

Including Tanya!

That was around the time Dev called Dean down to the front of the room. Which was when Elise had leaned over to Tanya and teased that her son had probably done it because Dean was sitting so close to her.

"There's no reason for you to leave, you know." Dev's cutting voice pulled her from her thoughts. "In case you're thinking I need help getting back to my Jeep."

"Of course you need help." She dismissed his words, chalking up his tone to his discomfort.

"No, I don't."

"Yes, you do." Geez, this man had cornered the market on stubbornness! Tanya tightened her grip on her purse. "So do you want to race to see who gets to the cars first? I can guarantee who'll win."

Dev's lips twitched. She wasn't sure if he was trying to hide his pain or a smile.

"Where are you parked?" he asked.

"In the lot behind the bakery. You?"

"Out on Main Street."

"Okay. We'll go to the Jeep first."

Dev took a step forward, once again invading her personal space. "I always make sure the lady gets to her car safe and sound."

Just as gallant as she'd guessed he'd be. "Well, this lady is ready to head home. Thanks for agreeing to be my escort."

She watched his eyes, seeing the exact moment Dev realized he'd been played.

He gestured to the door with the sweep of his hand. "After you, ma'am."

Tanya pointed across the room. "Aren't you going to say goodbye to your mother?"

Dev turned, seeking out his mother's gaze. It didn't take long for him to catch her attention because Elise Murphy was staring right at them. For how long, Tanya had no idea, but Dev gestured toward the door and his mother responded by blowing him a kiss.

Tanya then noticed Zip looking her way, so she sent him a quick wave. He winked at her before he went back to the game.

"You sure you're ready to leave?"

Dev's words took on a hard edge again, but Tanya only nodded. "Yep. Let's go."

They left the hall, and by the time they crossed the crowded parking lot and reached the sidewalk, a light rain had started to fall.

"Maybe you better go back inside. I can get my Jeep and drive you to your car."

She looked skyward, the mist cool and refreshing on her face and bare arms after the stuffiness of the people-packed church hall. "I'm not made of sugar. I won't melt."

"Yeah, well, maybe I will," Dev said.

"Hmm, I don't think so. You don't seem to be too sweet at the moment." Tanya made sure to keep her stride short, matching his slower pace. "What happened to your good mood?"

"It's gone."

"I can see that." His mood swings seemed to be connected to his soreness. Despite her mini acupressure lesson earlier, the hurt had to be rising again. "Are you in a lot of pain?"

"No."

"Was it being around your fellow firefighters?"

His footsteps faltered for a moment, but he kept on walking. "No."

Tanya knew she should just let it go. It was clear Dev wasn't in the mood to talk, but her concern for him got the better of her. "I only ask because I saw you speaking with the fire chief—"

"How did you know that's who he was?"

"Well, the uniform was a giveaway, but Dean told me."

His head snapped toward her, and even though she couldn't see his eyes—his hat was pulled low over his brow, casting a shadow over his face—she could feel the heat of his gaze.

"Dean told you?"

Wow, it felt as if the night's warm temperature had just

dropped a few degrees. "Yes, he said he's a member of the volunteer fire department, too," Tanya quickly explained. "Did you know that? He joined a few months ago, so he's still a probie. I think that's the word he used."

"Yeah, that's the right word. It means he's still in probationary training, and no, I didn't know he was on the squad."

"Dean thought you might've been talking to the chief about going back to work—"

"Actually, I told the chief I plan to resign from the department." Dev punched at the night air with the tip of his cane for emphasis. "What good is a firefighter who can barely get across the room without tripping over his feet? Not that I'm missed at the station. They've got themselves a couple of new recruits, Zip obviously being one of them."

He sounded angry, but Tanya could hear the hurt behind his words. It reminded her of the despair she'd felt when trusting her heart, not to mention her career and reputation, to one person—the wrong person—had resulted in her having to leave a job she'd loved, too.

Although after spending the weekend back home and driving by the clinic a few times, she'd come to understand that she missed the work far more than she missed her ex.

Who would've thought that?

"I'm sorry, Dev. I know what it's like to give up a job that's such a huge part of your identity."

"Yeah, well, I've got no one to blame for this but myself. I'm just surprised Zip waited so long to step up. We've been trying for a year to get him to join."

"So what did your chief say?" Tanya asked, her curiosity getting the better of her. "About your resignation?"

"He turned it down."

"Is that allowed?"

"Probably not, technically, but he said he wanted my help...with training."

Other than what she read in the newspaper or saw on the evening news, she didn't know much about what it took to be a fireman, but being in top physical condition had to be at the top of the list.

Dev definitely wasn't anymore.

Could he ever be that way again?

She'd seen people recover from injuries like his, with time and lots of hard work, and come back even stronger.

Then again, recent experience taught her there were also those who pushed themselves too hard, too fast and ended up with a permanent disability.

"What exactly does that mean?" she asked. "Helping with training?"

"Have you ever been to a firefighting competition?"

Tanya nodded. It'd been a few years, but the events were popular attractions each summer back home as teams competed in events that represented their daily lives as firefighters.

"Well, the team from the DFD is competing at the end of next month," Dev continued, "and the chief seems to think the rookies could use my help."

Concern welled up inside her. "Dev, you've come a long way since the accident, but you've still got a lot of recovering to do. A few PT sessions here and there and an hour doing water aerobics isn't enough for you to be taking on something so strenuous."

"I know I've been lax about my physical therapy over the past couple of months. But all that's changed. I saw Pete on Monday and we've upped my sessions to three times a week."

Meaning he'd been down in Laramie twice this week, including today, as there was no way his physical therapist would do the strenuous sessions on back-to-back days. "That's a good start, but you still can't—"

"Believe me, I'll well aware of what I can and cannot do." His tone was sharp and biting, but the deep sigh that followed took away the sting of his words.

She waited, wondering if he was going to bring up the two of them working together. He remained silent and kept walking, and this time Tanya was able to do the same, even if it required her biting down on her bottom lip.

When they got to the town square, they continued on past the gazebo, heading for the next block and the bakery's parking lot.

Most of the businesses were closed up for the night, their interiors dark except for a few that sported softly glowing lights inside. There were a few people still out and about, but the sidewalks were mainly empty.

As they walked, she put a bit of space between them, unable to stop the professional in her from observing him. Especially after what he'd just told her about working with the fire department again.

His boots offered a steady click against the cement, meaning he wasn't dragging his feet. There was a hitch in his step, but his grip on the cane was steady, much better than the white-knuckle way he'd held onto it back at the hall.

Her gaze traveled up to his hips, and she leaned back a bit, taking a moment to admire his Wranglers-clad backside.

Hey, she was only human!

The muscles in his arms were tense, standing out in stark relief, and he held his shoulders stiff beneath his cotton shirt, now clinging to his skin thanks to the light rain that had finally stopped.

On a scale of one to ten, she'd bet his pain level was probably a solid six or even creeping up to a seven.

As if finally noticing her gaze, he pulled the brim of his hat even lower over his eyes, making it almost impossible to see most his face, even with the street lights.

Still, the timeless style fit him perfectly and she envied how he wore the familiar Western fixture with familiarity and ease.

She'd never been a hat girl.

Even during the winter, she never liked wearing them, preferring earmuffs or the hood of her jacket. Learning to wear the extravagant headpieces during her showgirl days in Reno, never mind dancing in the darn things, had bothered her even more than the skimpy outfits.

"Why are you staring at me?"

Dev's question yanked Tanya from her daydreaming and she almost tripped over her feet.

Busted! Deciding not to tell him she was analyzing him, Tanya blurted out the first thing that popped into her head. "Could I ask you a favor?"

He glanced at her. "Sure."

Oh, this was crazy. "Forget it. It's not important."

"Tanya—"

"No, it's silly." She couldn't believe she'd even opened her mouth. The alley leading to the parking lot behind the bakery was just ahead, past the next shop. "Don't…don't worry about it."

Dev stopped in the middle of the sidewalk, this time standing in a pool of light from one of the ornate street lamps. "Tell me what you were going to ask me."

Tanya sighed. She should've known he wouldn't let this go. "Okay, this is going to sound trivial, but I was looking at you…and admiring your hat. I know it's hard to believe, seeing how I was born and raised in this part of the country, but I've never worn one. Never even tried one on. So I was wondering…"

He bumped up the brim and stared at her. "You want to try on my Stetson?"

Tanya smiled, lifting her shoulders in a little shrug and feeling more ridiculous by the moment. "I told you it was silly."

He lifted it off his head and held it out to her.

A childish thrill raced through her. "Really?"

"It'll probably be too big for you, but sure, go ahead."

She took the hat, surprised at the weight and the warmth of the felt material, despite the dampness from tonight's weather. "Are there any special instructions?"

That got her a smile, his first since he'd called that last game of bingo. "Put it on the same way I took it off, by the brim. Don't grab the crown. That'll only warp the shape."

Tanya nodded and flipping the hat over, plopped it on her head. But it sat off center. "Oh! Darn ponytail."

She took the hat off again and with one hand easily slid her hair free of the elastic band. The long strands fell past her shoulders as she shook her head back and forth.

The sound of Dev clearing his throat made her stop midshake. "What?"

"That's the first time I've ever seen you with your hair down."

"Really?" She thought back to the times they'd spent together. At Mac's, his physical therapy session and lunch afterwards, the fitness center and today. "Yeah, I do tend to wear it up most of the time. Keeps it out of the way."

"Well, it looks good…down."

A heated blush filled her face at his words. She was glad she was standing in the shadows. "Thanks."

Trying again, Tanya put the hat on. Yes, it was a bit too big and as heavy on her as she'd expected. The material had captured Devlin's body heat, not to mention his scent, and both enveloped her. She closed her eyes for a moment, enjoying the sensation.

"Tanya?"

Her eyes flew open. "Oh! Um, I wonder what I look…"

She whirled around, saw that they were standing in front of Fay's Flower Shop. She hurried over to the large window, able to see her reflection in the glass. "Hey, this isn't half bad."

Turning first to the left and then the right, she liked what she saw. Maybe she should finally get herself one. Not in the dark color of Dev's, but perhaps one made of straw. She'd seen plenty of ladies in town wearing them.

Not that she'd have much use for it walking the streets of London once she left, but it'd be a nice reminder of Destiny—

"Tanya?"

She blinked and turned around, realizing he'd said her name more than once. "I'm sorry. What did you say?"

"I asked if you'd do me a favor now."

His softly spoken words sent a shiver through her that she quickly blamed on the night air. "Ah, sure. What is it?"

"Stay away from Zip."

As soon as he'd spoken, Dev wished he'd kept his big mouth shut.

It'd been a long night. He was tired, hurting and so damn jealous of his buddy and the way he'd winked at Tanya just before they'd left the church hall, he couldn't see straight.

Then to learn the man had pretty much taken his place at the firehouse was a blow he hadn't had the chance to deal with yet. Hearing Tanya say he was in no shape to train anyone, even if it was just for a fun competition, had been the final straw.

Everything she'd told him had been true, but dammit, it wasn't like he planned to become an official member of the team.

Hell, he didn't even plan to attend the competition.

He just wanted to be able to walk into the firehouse without needing this damn cane because there was no way he could turn down the chief's request.

"Stay away from—" Confusion laced her words and colored her features. "You mean Dean? Why?"

"He's a player. Dates a different woman every month. Every week. Trust me, the man isn't interested in anything but a short-term fling."

Her shoulders went rigid and her mouth pressed into a hard line.

Wrong thing to say.

Talk about going from the frying pan into the fire. Hell, he'd just pulled the rookie mistake of walking into a blaze without bothering to make sure he had a full tank of compressed air.

Or in his case, common sense.

Yeah, he'd been stupid to assume that she'd even think about getting involved with Dean. Especially after the way they'd kissed just a week ago.

Even though she'd told him she wasn't interested in getting involved, the way her mouth had moved under his told a different story—

"Oh, that's funny, coming from you." She jerked his hat off her head and held it out to him. "Your family made it clear that you and Zip used to run neck and neck for the title of Destiny's busiest bachelor."

He tried to concentrate on her words, but the sight of

the long dark strands of her hair whipping over her shoulders took him back to another time.

Another place.

When she'd emerged after changing out of her sexy showgirl costume wearing an even sexier little black dress, her hair had been loose and flowing, even longer than she wore it now. The ends had reached the soft swells of her breasts, curling just enough to draw his gaze—

She shook the Stetson at him, breaking up the memory. He took it, easily flipping the hat over and settling it back on his head, automatically yanking the brim low again.

"I'm not like that. Not anymore."

"Who says I'm looking for anything? You know, just because a woman is single and unattached doesn't mean she's searching for company from a man. Present company included." Tanya flipped open her purse and dug out her keys. "I have no idea how this conversation went from your health issues to my dating habits, but I think I can safely get to my car from here. Goodnight, Dev."

She turned away and headed for the alley, but then looked over her shoulder at him, eyes snapping with fire. "On the other hand, I'm only in town for another six weeks. Maybe something short-term is just what I'm looking for. I'll be sure to keep Zip in mind."

She made it three steps into the alley before he caught up to her, wrapping one arm around her waist.

Letting out a yelp of surprise, she spun around. Dev used the move to easily pull her up hard against his body.

"Dev! What are you doing?" She grabbed at his arms. "Be careful of your leg!"

"If you're serious about looking for company, you don't have to go any farther. My name should be right at the top of your list."

Tanya went lax in his arms. "We've been over this already."

"Are you telling me that you don't feel whatever this crazy thing is between us every time we're together?" He bumped up the brim of his hat with the handle of his cane before dropping it back to his side. With one step, he pressed her against the brick wall before he leaned in close. "From the moment I saw you at Mac's I knew there was something special about you. And that was long before I kissed you. Again."

Tanya flattened her hands against his chest, her keys still in her grasp. The heat of her touch through his damp shirt started his heart pounding, and he was sure she could feel his reaction beneath her fingertips.

"Dev, I'm sorry. Sorry about what I said last week in the changing room. I never should've just blurted out like that about us in Reno—"

"Are you kidding me?" He cut her off, surprised by her regret. Leaning back in order to look her in the eye, he continued, his voice softer now. "If anyone should apologize for what happened—for what didn't happen— between us that night, it should be me."

"Oh, please. It was a long time ago."

"What about last week?" Dev pressed forward, holding her in place with his body, his hips and thighs lost in the folds of her skirt. He released her waist, moving to sink his fingers into her hair. "I'll admit I kissed you first, something I wanted to do from the first moment we met, but it didn't take long for you to kiss me back."

Tanya's tongue slipped out to glide over her lips. Was she remembering that kiss?

Dev's gaze dropped to her mouth and his head dipped lower. A low groan filled the space between them, and he honestly didn't know if it came from her or him.

He wanted to kiss her again. He wanted to feel the heat of her mouth under his.

Again.

It would be easy.

She was willing, he could see it in her eyes, feel it in the way she arched against his arousal where it surged against her belly.

Then he felt a faint twinge, nothing too bad, but it was enough to make him catch his breath for a moment as it raced across his back. He closed his eyes, refusing to let her see his discomfort, but he was too late.

"Dev, let me help you. I want to do all I can to make that pain go away forever." Tanya's words came out in a heated plea, her fingers fisting his shirt. "You might not get back to being a firefighter again, but your life would be so much better. But I've told you I don't get involved with people I work with."

Pulling a deep breath only filled his head with her sexy yet sweet scent, but he did it anyway, needing the moment to gather his thoughts.

He then opened his eyes again, relieved to find the sharp stab of pain gone. "I thought we already settled that. I fired you, remember?"

Her mouth dropped open in surprise. "I thought you were kidding."

"I wasn't."

"Why?"

"Because I want you."

There, he said it.

Four simple words that spoke a simple truth.

He hadn't wanted to be with a woman in a long time, even after he'd been physically able to.

For a while he worried his lack of desire for female company was a side effect of the trauma he'd gone through. He'd even mentioned it to his therapist during one of their sessions when Pete had tried to distract him by talking about his own obsession with an A-list movie star, but the man had assured Dev that when the time was right, his body would respond.

But it was more than a physical reaction.

Something about this woman had touched a place deeper inside of him. It was almost like he'd been waiting for her.

"Oh, Dev, you don't want me." Tanya shook her head. "You want a memory."

"Tanya, I hate to admit this, but the memories of that night in Reno are hazy at best. Snatches really. I remember your dress, your hair." His fingers, still tangled in the silky lengths, tightened into a gentle fist. "Especially now that I've seen it down. You wore it longer back then, didn't you?"

She nodded.

"Yeah, I remember wrapping it around my hand as I pulled you—"

"Dev, please." Tanya laid the tips of her fingers over his mouth. They trembled against his lips for a moment before she snatched them away. "I thought...I thought you wanted my help with your recovery."

He smiled, noticing she hadn't shot down his assertion. "I want that, too."

Her lips twitched as if she was holding back a smile of her own. He swore if the tip of her tongue came out to wet those lips one more time, he was going to take another kiss, permission be damned.

"Selfish much?" she asked.

"For three days last year I thought I might die. Being selfish is okay sometimes."

Dev was surprised he'd actually said those words aloud.

His brother Nolan had said the being selfish part when he'd stopped by Dev's office last week to talk about the ongoing situation with the helicopter, which was due to be delivered any day now.

"Have you ever heard that song 'You Can't Always Get What You Want'?"

"Sure, but it isn't a question of what I want, it's what I need," he shot back. Deciding to back off for the moment, Dev put a bit of space between them. The last thing he wanted was to scare her off, especially now that he knew how much he did need her.

In more ways than one.

"Right now I need to work on getting better. I told you about my PT sessions, but I want to include your idea of aquatic therapy in my recovery. That class with the grandmas was tough, but not taxing. I want to do more of it."

"But you told your mother you weren't going back to the fitness center."

"No, what I have in mind is working out in my family's pool. It's in ground, heated and best of all, private. Or as private as it can be considering the size of my family and the fact that someone is always around. I've talked this over with my physical therapist, who agrees it's a good idea. I've also done some research online about the variety of workouts that can be done in a pool and—"

"Dev, aquatic therapy isn't something you should try on your own. One wrong move and you could do some serious damage."

"So come over and help me out. Just as friends."

"Friends?"

Dev's mouth rose in a smile. "For now."

Chapter Ten

She wasn't coming. She wasn't coming. She wasn't coming.

The mantra played over and over inside Dev's head as his body cut through the warm water of the family pool. He'd finished loosening up and was now on lap number twelve, which wasn't saying much as he was only going from side to side in the shallow end.

Even after a week of intensive pool work he didn't trust himself not to get into trouble in the deep end if he swam the entire length of the pool.

Still, it felt good to do the standard crawl stroke instead of that paltry breaststroke Tanya had insisted he start with.

He stretched one arm overhead before slicing back into the water in a rhythmic motion, then switched to the other arm, back and forth, back and forth.

Any discomfort through his shoulders was barely noticeable, as long as he didn't stay at this for very long.

Due to the width of the pool, he only completed about three complete arm cycles before his fingertips touched the opposite wall and he headed back the other way, but it was enough.

For now.

She wasn't coming. She wasn't coming. She wasn't coming.

Deep down, he knew that wasn't true.

Tanya was dedicated to helping him. They'd been working together for the past ten days, except for Tuesday when they were rained out and yesterday when he'd been at the hospital all day getting scheduled tests to track his progress.

So why did he think she wouldn't show up?

Because the chant was a superstitious ritual he'd gotten used to practicing daily to ensure that she would.

Yeah, he didn't quite understand the logic, either.

"Hey, I thought the object of you being in there was to work."

Dev turned around.

Liam stood next to the pool, dressed casually in jeans and a ratty T-shirt, a tool belt hung low on his hips and dark sunglasses shading his eyes from the sun. Unlike Dev, the man hadn't bothered to shave, seeing how it was Saturday, and was looking a little scruffy.

Then again, Liam wasn't hoping to have a beautiful woman show up any minute.

"I am working," Dev shot back, even though he'd been standing on the far side of the pool, lost in thought. "You playing handyman today?"

Liam nodded, jerking his head toward his place down by the lake. "The exterior is finally done and the inside walls are up, but I want to do most of the electrical work myself."

"Company president, certified electrician and a former rodeo star. Geez, bro, you do it all. I'd like to help," he said, offering a simple shrug. A pain-free shrug. Maybe Tanya's suggestions really were paying off. "But you know how it is."

"Yeah, I know. You've got a sexy *Baywatch* babe on the way."

Dev smiled, thinking about the red one-piece swimsuit Tanya wore when they worked in the pool. It was modest by most standards, but with her toned body, long legs and tiny waist, she looked just like a character from that beachy lifeguard show from his youth.

"If she shows up," he said, his grin slipping a bit as he kept his tone light. She'd never been this late before. "So am I going to have an audience again today? Katie and Laurie actually took their lunch break out on the deck yesterday."

"Yeah, I saw them sitting out here. I planned to join them but got caught on a conference call," Liam said. "Nolan just left with the kids. Abby is heading to the library and the twins have a ball game. The folks are around, but Dad said he's going to give me a hand. I'm sure Mom will be taking a seat on the deck to watch."

What else was new? It made it tough, but not impossible, to lay on the charm while being chaperoned. "Great."

His brother moved to the edge of the pool and crouched, making a motion with his hand that he wanted Dev to move closer.

Dev complied, heading across the pool, enjoying the heat of the sun on his bare back.

Thanks to regaining some of his muscle tone, he'd decided to lose the wet shirt a couple of days ago. Not that enjoying the feel of Tanya's hands on his bare skin had anything to do with his decision.

Or the appreciative look in her eyes when he caught her staring.

The first time, he'd started to explain away the scars, but Tanya waved off his words, telling him they were hardly noticeable.

That was a lie, but he'd liked hearing it.

"So what's up?" he asked, noticing how his brother's good-natured smile had disappeared. "You got serious all of a sudden."

Liam yanked his glasses off and tucked them on top of his head. "The new helo arrived yesterday. The mechanics at the airstrip have given the all clear. Bryant and Laurie are taking it for an inaugural flight today."

Trying to ignore the hard lump that formed in his stomach, Dev pulled in a deep breath through his nose and nodded. "Thanks for letting me know."

He and the rest of family had declared a truce about the new helicopter since he'd stormed out of Liam's office a couple of weeks ago. But he still wasn't happy about his brothers flying, even if he'd accepted there was nothing he could do about it.

Just like they'd accepted that nothing they said was going to get him behind the controls again.

"Bry said they'd probably fly over the house. We didn't want you to be surprised by that."

Dev nodded again, pushing off from the side of the pool to float backward toward the center. "Yeah, okay."

Liam stared at him for a moment and Dev thought he was going to say something more, but then he rose to his full height, putting his glasses back in place. "Hey, make sure you tell Tanya if she decides to give another yoga class, I might join in."

His brother's words surprised Dev and he stopped his underwater hand motions. Sinking quickly, he put his feet down, but not before catching a mouthful of water. He choked, spitting it out as Liam laughed.

"Careful, bro. You're supposed to swim in that stuff, not drink it."

Dev shot his brother a look as he remembered the unplanned yoga class Tanya had given when their aquatic therapy was rained out last Tuesday.

There were six women, including his mother and two women who were clients of the company, in town to discuss vacation homes, who couldn't find a yoga class scheduled at the fitness center. Tanya's impromptu session had quickly become the talk of the office.

"Maybe I should put off my plans, change into my swim trunks and join you two," Liam continued. "Not that I need any therapy, but that girl can certainly rock a bathing suit—"

"Hey!" Dev angled his hand into the water with a sharp whack, sending a generous splash of water in his brother's direction. "Murphy rule number 9! You're not allowed to think about Tanya with her clothes off. You're not even allowed to think about her when she's fully clothed."

"I guess it's too late to say the same thing to you."

The deep voice behind him had Dev spinning around, the move causing a familiar twinge across his back.

Mac stood at the pool's edge, wearing cargo shorts and a Hawaiian print shirt so bright Dev wished he'd grabbed his shades before getting into the water.

A quick look around told him Tanya was nowhere to be seen.

"Hey, Mac. What are you doing here?"

"Playing lifeguard?" Mac kicked off his shoes, sat on the pool's edge and dropped his legs into the water. "Geez, this is supposed to be cool and refreshing. The water is hotter than my morning java."

"It's that way on purpose," Dev said.

"Hey, Mac," Liam called from his side of the pool.

Mac offered a wave in return and Dev glanced over his shoulder, but his brother was already heading across the yard toward his log home.

Glad when the painful twinges of a minute ago didn't reappear, Dev made his way over to his friend and propped his arms on the side of the pool. "So, did you come by for a reason?"

"That piece of junk Tanya drives is giving her trouble again, so I offered to bring her over."

She's here.

Heat radiated through Dev's chest that had nothing to do with the water's temperature. He straightened and braced his hands on his hips, trying to appear casual. "Ah, then where is she?"

"Inside," Mac said, jerking his thumb at the house, "dropping off a couple of her fruit smoothies to your mother."

Milkshakes laced with a bunch of Chinese herbs. No, thanks.

Dev had to admit the first time she'd offered him one overloaded with pineapple, it had looked good. But once she'd rattled off the list of ingredients, he took a pass no matter how hard she'd tried to persuade him that the herbs didn't taste bad and weren't addictive.

"She says you're making a lot of progress." Mac drew his dark sunglasses down to the tip of his nose and peered at Dev over the top edge. "Are you? Making progress?"

Dev could tell from the older man's tone that he wasn't talking about his physical health. "Look, I know you overheard that crack I made to Liam about thinking about Tanya in a certain state of undress—"

"Yeah, like I said, it's probably too late to ask you to follow that same rule, huh?"

"We're just—"

"Friends." Mac cut him off again. "Yeah, she's shoveling the same load of…er, bull."

"What? You don't believe her?"

"Her? I guess so. You? No way. I know you too well."

Dev frowned. "Yeah, well, other than working with her right here in this pool—with plenty of adult supervision most days—we haven't spent any time together."

"Not for lack of trying on your part," Mac pointed out, pushing his sunglasses back into place. "Dinner, movies, a drive in the country."

Dev wasn't sure what bothered him more. The fact that Tanya kept turning him down whenever he asked her out on a date or that she was sharing all of this with his buddy.

Who also happened to be her grandfather.

Okay, he was bothered more by her negative responses. "All of which she's turned down with a very polite 'no, thanks.'"

"She went to bingo the other night for the second time."

"Yeah, just me, her and the rest of Destiny."

He and Tanya had sat with his mom and her crew while Zip played master of ceremonies for the evening.

Granted, the guy had checked with him first.

Attending training sessions with the fire department's competition team out at the fairgrounds earlier in the week and finding Zippenella on the team hadn't surprised him. He'd waited for a comment about Tanya from the guy, but Zip been all business as the team practiced for the various events while Dev offered suggestions to the rookies and controlled the stop watch.

Not exactly the way he'd wanted to be part of the team, but he had to admit it'd been great to be with the crew again. Even if they were already pushing him to join them at the competition as an honorary member.

He couldn't do it. He couldn't stand there, even without the cane that he hadn't used once in the past four days, and watch his friends do what he'd excelled at this time last year.

"Tanya got a package in the mail yesterday. From that fancy school she's going to next month."

Mac's words brought Dev back to the here and now. "Oh, yeah? Good for her."

"Lots of information about classes and stuff. But she also found out the girl she was going to room with has backed out. The school is trying to find someone else, but there are no guarantees."

"That's too bad." Unable to take the sun's rays reflecting off the water and the rainbow of colors on Mac's shirt any longer, Dev motioned for his sunglasses on a nearby table. "I'm sure she'll get it figured out between now and the end of June."

His buddy leaned back, grabbed the glasses and tossed them in his direction. "You're okay with her going?"

Dev had to backpedal a few steps to catch them, but he still paused for a moment before answering and then sliding them on. "Why wouldn't I be?"

"You tell me."

Folding his arms across his chest, Dev pulled in a deep breath and slowly released it, despite his clenched jaw. He should've figured this was coming. He and Mac had run into each other a few times, but they hadn't spoken about Tanya since that first day.

Why Mac felt it necessary to issue his warning again, Dev didn't know. He thought they'd both said their piece the first time around. "Just because we're friends—"

"And you're trying to be friendlier—"

"Look, I know how important that school is to her. I know she's wanted to go there ever since she became a licensed acupuncturist." Dev made his way back through the water until he stood next to his buddy, his fingers biting into the heated flagstone that rimmed the sides of the pool. "I know firsthand how great she is at everything she does, except the needle stuff of course, but don't think I haven't noticed how much better your hands have looked since she's been sticking you on a daily basis."

"That's true," Mac said, curling his fingers into easy fists.

"I also know she got into this business thanks to falling off the stage and injuring her back during her showgirl days, how her last boyfriend treated her like crap after she lost her job, on Christmas Eve no less, that she wants to own an orange calico cat someday just because she thinks they're pretty and her obsession with Justin Timber-whoever started back when he was part of…In Tune or whatever they were called."

Dev paused to catch his breath, letting the silence build. There was a ton of other things about Tanya that he could share, both important and insignificant, thanks to her natural ability to distract him from the pain during the first couple of sessions with senseless chatter.

But soon their talks had changed from discussing the weather and her favorite music to sharing memories of their childhood to their plans for the future.

"Your point is?"

"We are friends, Mac. I like her and I think she likes me. If we become anything else during the rest of her stay in Destiny, it's no one's business but ours."

Dev held out his hand. "I need you to be okay with that because you and I are still going to be friends once she heads across the pond." The thought of her going anywhere, though, twisted his gut. "Right?"

Mac stared at Dev's outstretched hand for a moment, then took it in a strong handshake that showed just how much Tanya's treatments had helped his arthritis. "Okay, we're good. I just got worried because of some of the things she was saying last night."

About him? About them? Intrigued, Dev couldn't help but ask, "What was that?"

"I don't know, it wasn't anything specific. This roommate snafu is bugging her, especially if she's going to have to pay for the flat, I think she called it, by herself. I'm planning to send her off with a sizable check if I can get away with it."

"What does that mean?"

"When I told how much I was giving her, she got upset and insisted I only pay her the regular hourly rate." Mac paused, then peered at him again over the top of his sunglasses. "She did mention she's been helping you out as a friend, not an employee, so I'm guessing you aren't paying her."

"That's right. But that doesn't mean I can't help out, as well. As a friend." An idea started to form and Dev couldn't believe he hadn't thought of it until now. "The business has some contracts in the UK, especially now that Ian Somersby, that Scottish actor Liam met last month, is definitely interested in us building his log mansion on land outside of Castle Douglas in the south of Scotland."

"So?"

"Maybe I can find her a place in London. Something close to the school, but still affordable. Hell, I could write it off as a business expense and she wouldn't owe me anything."

"That's a great idea," Mac said. "But I don't know. Tanya might not like it."

"Why?" The more Dev thought about this, the better it sounded. "I mean, it's the least I can do. She's helping me, I can help her. It's no big deal—"

"Oh, really?" The feminine voice came from behind him, cutting off his words. "It sure sounds like a big deal to me."

Tanya's trained eye caught the moment every muscle in Dev's body stilled as he heard her speak. He had plenty of them, and the more he worked out, both in the pool and with his physical therapist, the more sculpted the man became.

Putting back on the weight he'd lost, in a good way, was doing wonders for his body, and since he'd started spending more and more time out in the sun, his skin had turned golden brown despite her constantly harping on how he should use sunscreen.

Standing in the shallow end of the pool, thanks to the light blue swim trunks he usually wore and the way the sun danced on top of the waist-high water, the man actually appeared naked at first glance.

Yowza!

He'd never gotten that far that night in Reno. Although he had looked mighty fine wearing nothing but a pair of unzipped jeans that barely clung to his lanky frame and allowed a glimpse of black briefs.

But still…

Hands on his hips, Devlin slowly turned around, dark sunglasses shading his blue eyes. Not that she needed to see them to guess they held the same guilty expression as her grandfather's for her finding the two of them discussing her financial issues.

Mac hastily got to his feet and shoved his sandals back on, making ready for a quick getaway. Smart man.

"Elise invited the two of us to stay for a barbecue this afternoon." She spoke directly to her grandfather. "I told her you had some errands to run, but you'd be back. Around three?"

"Uh, sure." Mac nodded while backing away from the pool to the grassy area. "I'll be here. Thank Elise for me, and Dev... Good luck, man."

"Deserting a buddy when he's in the line of fire?" Dev deadpanned under his breath. "Thanks a lot."

Mac only grinned, holding his hands wide in mock surrender before giving a quick wave and heading for his truck.

Tanya waited until she had Dev's full attention again before she walked to the nearby table and set down the water bottles she'd brought out from the kitchen.

"Look, Tanya, I didn't mean to..."

Keeping her back to him, she ignored his words while tucking her thumbs into the waistband of her yoga pants. One quick push and they were past her hips and backside. A thrill raced through her when Dev's voice trailed off to nothing as he apparently lost the ability to speak.

She gave a little wiggle and the pants shimmied to the patio. She stepped out of the material gathered around her feet and then unzipped her lightweight jacket, letting it slide past her shoulders to catch on the tips of her fingers for a moment. Taking her time, she slipped out of her sandals and laid her clothes on one of the lounge chairs.

"Ah, you...you look..." Dev's words were short, sweet and barely above a whisper. "Wow."

Just the reaction she'd been hoping for. And she hadn't even turned around yet.

To think she'd been nervous about wearing this suit

today, and even more nervous about putting her let's-get-to-know-each-other-a-little-better plan into action.

The other night she'd called a couple of girlfriends back in Colorado Springs, and during their three-way chat that had covered everything from jobs to families to men, she'd finally told them about Dev.

When they'd insisted on visuals, she'd sent a link to his page on the Murphy Mountain Log Home website that had two great pictures. A more formal one in which he looked amazing in a suit and tie, with just a hint of that killer smile of his, while the other was more casual, taken on a job site where he rocked the flannel shirt, jeans and work boots look.

After much discussion, her friends had convinced her she was crazy for holding this guy at arm's length.

She liked him. He liked her. Why not do a short-term, let's-have-fun-while-it-lasts kind of hookup?

Did she really want to get to London and be forced to live with regrets over what might have been?

Go for it, her friends had urged.

Tanya had finally agreed. The next time she saw Dev, she'd be the one asking for a date. Still, switching gears on him, from turning him down every time he'd asked her out to her now doing the asking—

What if he said no just to spite her?

That's when she'd decided a kick-ass bathing suit instead of her standard lifeguard-style one-piece was the reinforcement she needed. She'd spent the day shopping for the perfect one and had come out here ready to put her plan into action.

Shoulders back, posture straight, sunglasses on, Tanya slowly turned around, giving him the full effect.

This suit was still a one-piece, but black, with a halter-style top that tied around her neck. The front plunged to show off lots of skin and curves, with only three tiny silver buckles keeping the material snug over her breasts. There was full coverage across her backside—this was his family's pool after all—but the low, scooped back was very sexy.

Yeah, the way Dev's mouth fell open and snapped shut—twice—was exactly the effect she'd been hoping for.

Until she'd overheard him talking to Mac about doing her a favor.

She's helping me. I can help her.

Familiar words. The same ones spoken a few years ago by someone else who'd *said* he'd wanted to help when she found herself in a tight financial situation and needed to pay for some job training.

An offer that supposedly had no strings attached.

She'd taken Ross at his word that day and accepted his assistance, only to have him throw how much money he'd given her back in her face when he ended things between them.

So now, instead of a flirtatious beginning to her and Dev's session—one which would end with them making more intimate plans for tonight—she was switching gears.

Tanya was determined not to let him do her any favors. She wasn't taking any chances. She'd found out the hard way that favors tended to come with strings attached.

It had cost her dearly last time, but she'd finally cut the last of her ties to Ross, and there was no way she was going to get tangled up like that again.

Chapter Eleven

Grabbing a tube of sunscreen, Tanya walked to the stairs that led down into the water. She perched on the top step, next to the foam resistance dumbbells Dev used during their workouts.

She tossed first one, and then the other, at him. "It looks like you're done with your warm-up and laps. Why don't you get started on your arm exercises while I put on some lotion?"

Dev caught the weights as they landed in front of him with a splash. "Why do I get the feeling you aren't interested in talking to me?"

"I am talking to you." Tanya squirted a large dollop of cream into the palm of her hand. Angling one leg along the edge of the pool, she smoothed the lotion on, starting at her toes and slowly—very slowly—working her way upward.

"Tanya—"

"Your mother said your family is going to descend on

the backyard in less than three hours. Do you want to be this afternoon's entertainment?"

His silence was the answer.

"Okay, then. Go ahead and get started without me."

Dev muttered something under his breath and began the familiar routine. She watched him work as she finished with her legs, wordlessly evaluating the ease with which he moved his upper body. It really was amazing how far he had come in just the past ten days.

That's when she came to a decision. Despite her worries over his conversation with Mac, she was still interested in getting a little closer to this man.

She just had to be smart about it.

With that in mind, she concentrated on coating her arms and chest with lotion, biting down on her bottom lip when one of the weights slipped from Dev's hand the exact moment her fingertips dipped into the bodice's edge of her suit.

What? She had to make sure every inch of her exposed cleavage was protected from the sun.

Properly lathered, she sat and enjoyed the warmth of the sun and the gentle breeze across her skin for a moment longer, knowing the pool water wasn't going to be very refreshing at its current temperature.

And yes, she was aware that Dev hadn't taken his eyes off her.

At least it looked that way, unless he had his eyes closed behind his dark shades.

Deciding it was time to join him in the pool, Tanya stood and walked down the steps. Dev paused, but she motioned for him to continue the workout as she moved through the water toward him.

They remained quiet for the next half hour as he finished the upper body exercises.

"Okay, good. Now, the lower. Left leg, standard reps. Right leg, don't stop until I tell you."

Dev only sighed, but handed over the weights to her.

She moved to the edge of the pool and tossed them up onto the flagstone. Turning back, she watched his movements closely, again noting how easily he transitioned from position to position, cranking out the required number of repetitions for each move without a hint of strain or discomfort.

"How are you feeling?" she asked, just to be sure. "Any pain anywhere?"

"Nope. I'm fi—" He stopped, a hint of a grin lifting one corner of his mouth. He must be remembering how she'd told him that using that particular word drove her nuts. "I'm doing okay. Physically."

"Meaning you're having issues mentally?"

"Meaning it's damn hard to concentrate with you in that swimsuit."

Hmm, mission accomplished.

She moved out of his line of sight to observe from both the side and back, acknowledging her own focus was none too steady at the moment, either.

Now that she'd decided to take things up a notch, spend some time together away from the pool, could she go through with it?

Could she ask him out on a date and not have him think—?

"You're mad at me, aren't you?"

Tanya pushed her sweaty bangs out of her face with the back of her hand, sending her dark sunglasses askew as she moved back around in front of him. Righting them, she tried to ignore Dev's smile.

"Wow, I can't even see your eyes, but it's suddenly kind

of chilly here in this ninety-plus-degree pool." He made an exaggerated shudder.

Tanya crossed her arms over her chest. She couldn't see Dev's eyes, either, but she'd bet they weren't on her face at the moment. "What makes you think I'm mad?"

"Cause if you make me do one more side leg lift I think I can forget about the cane and just go right for a wheelchair."

She shoved her glasses up on top of her head. "That's not funny."

"Who's kidding?" He huffed, his grin slipping a bit. "I get that the bum leg needs more attention, but I'm in the high sixties for reps on this side."

"Why didn't you say something? Please stop."

Dev ended his exercise, removed his sunglasses and slipped completely beneath the water.

She didn't react, other than to plant her hands on her hips. Not even when her silent count that had started the moment he disappeared reached one eighty. He'd done this to her during their first session, proving that thanks to his firefighting training he could hold his breath for almost three minutes.

She, on the other hand, had just about panicked, thinking the worst before he finally came back to the surface with a burst of—

Tanya jumped when his strong hands settled over hers, trapping them against her hips before he slowly ascended from the water just inches from her.

"What are you—?" She made an attempt at freeing herself, but the strength of Dev's grasp and the position of his feet on either side of hers kept her firmly in place. "What do you think you're doing?"

He looked down at her and her breath caught in her throat.

He was devastatingly handsome with his dark hair slicked back against his skull. The eyelashes framing his beautiful blue eyes were spiky and water dripped from the hard angles of his jaw and chin to land on her face and chest.

Her lips parted so she could breathe again and his head dipped a fraction of an inch, but no farther.

"Getting to the bottom of whatever it is that's bugging you."

"What makes you think—" Tanya relented, then sighed. "Okay, something is bugging me. Your offer to do me a favor just…rubbed me the wrong way."

"Yeah, I sort of figured that out. Do you want to tell me why, exactly?"

Talking about her ex and everything he'd cost her was the last thing she wanted to do right now. "Not really. Let's just say I let someone do me a favor once and it came back to haunt me in a big way."

"I was only trying to help, Tanya." His words were soft and low. "Mac mentioned your roommate situation and I just didn't want you to have any issues that would keep you from going to London as you planned."

The sincerity in his gaze, and in his voice, created a flutter in her belly. "Why?"

"Because you're truly talented at your craft. Take it from someone who once was a major skeptic about anything related to that hocus-pocus stuff. What you do, the way you help people…" He paused for a moment, his eyes darkening as he gazed at her. "The way you've helped me. I had given up on recovering any further, deciding the pain I was living with was a necessary evil. Maybe even someone's way of telling me that I deserved everything I got for the crash being my fault."

Horror that he'd been carrying that belief around inside of him filled her. "Oh, Dev, please don't think that. You didn't cause the accident."

"Maybe." His eyes took on a faraway look for a moment. Then he blinked and it was gone. His smile returned. "But back to you. Your studies are important and I think you should be able to concentrate on them and not have to worry about where you'll live. That's all I was trying to do."

"Thank you. Everything you said about me helping you... It really means a lot to me." She returned his smile, and tried to lighten the mood by saying, "Even if you won't let me share my favorite source of healing with you."

He released her and took a step back. "I know you keep hoping I'll change my mind about a pincushion session, but it's not going to happen."

"It's okay." Was it crazy that she missed the strong grip of his hands? "You've come so far in just the past couple of weeks. You've been working hard, Dev, and it shows."

"Thanks." He smiled. "So please just think about what I said. I'm on the phone with the UK all the time, so it would only take a quick call—"

"Thanks, but no. I'll handle things on my own."

"Suit yourself." His dimples deepened as his grin took on a roguish quality. "Hey, just think, if you'd come out a few minutes later you wouldn't have overheard me at all."

Oh, the Wonder Woman inside of her still wanted to wipe that devilish smirk right off his face.

Ask him on a date! That'll do it!

She started past him, sinking into the water to her shoulders and pushing off with her feet toward the stairs. The session was over and they both needed to shower and change clothes before the afternoon's festivities got started.

It was now or never.

"I've heard there's a double feature of campy horror flicks showing at the drive-in." She tossed the words out in what she hoped was a casual tone.

Dev, who'd been swimming beside her, stopped. "Huh?"

"There's a new drive-in theater down in Laramie." Tanya flipped over on her back, using her arms to stay afloat as she moved farther away from him. "Actually, it's an old drive-in that closed down about twenty-five years ago, but the new owners put a ton of money into renovations. I read that it's become very popular since it opened the beginning of May."

Boy, could I be any more chatty? Just say it!

"Anyway, I was planning to ask if you were interested in going tonight."

"You *were* planning to ask me? But you're not going to now?"

"I don't know. I wouldn't want to get in the way of any international business you might have to take care of— Oh!"

Dev had caught up with her just as she'd neared the stairs. Wrapping his arms around her waist, he easily maneuvered her to the side of the pool with the built-in hot tub.

Surrounded by stacks of flagstone, it sat higher than the rest of the pool in a small alcove hidden from view of the house and the outside deck.

With the two of them still shoulder deep in water, he backed her into the corner and braced his hands on either side of her against the flagstone edge. He slipped one bent knee between hers, and the shock of skin against skin had her grabbing onto his shoulders.

"Dev, what are you doing? Your family might see us."

"No one is outside. Ask me," he said in that low whisper of his that never failed to send shivers down her spine. "Ask me, Tanya."

"Devlin Murphy, would you like to go out—?"

His mouth covered hers, taking the rest of her words in a searing kiss. That flutter in her belly exploded in a riot of desire, sexual hunger and need.

Her hands slid up around his neck and she angled her head, deepening their connection as she returned his kiss.

Seconds later, he started to caress her lower back with one of his hands, pulling her closer until she was pressed against every hard inch of him.

He took her mouth again and again, his tongue boldly sweeping in and playing with hers, kissing her with a toe-curling resolve that she matched with equal passion.

It was as if they wanted to make up for wasted time.

But it hadn't been wasted.

Yes, her initial attraction to him had been based on a long-ago memory of a shared night of physical desire. What else could it have been, as they'd known so little about each other?

But now...now she knew him.

She knew his strength and humor in overcoming his personal demons. Admired his loyalty to both his family's business and his volunteer work. Respected his newfound dedication in recovering from an event that could've taken his life.

An event that almost had.

Even though he'd physically survived, the accident last summer had taken something from Devlin, something deep inside, a sense of self-worth that he was finding again.

Thanks to her. At least according to him.

That thought caused the sting of tears to press against

her eyelids. She squeezed them shut as he broke their kiss, tracing her jaw with his lips until he reached her ear.

"I lost you," he whispered against her skin. "Where did you go?"

His question brought her out of the fog created by what a remarkable man she'd come to find Dev was. "I'm right here."

"Yes, you are. Finally."

It took some doing, but Tanya finally convinced him they had to get out of the water. Neither one of them knew the exact time, but she was sure they were going to be overrun with Murphys at any moment.

Dev couldn't have cared less.

He had held her in his arms and kissed her, with the promise of more to come now that they were at last going on a date.

And it'd been at her invitation.

He watched her walk up the pool steps in front of him, the water streaming from her curves in a way that made his mouth water. The new swimsuit fit her perfectly, but he wasn't entirely sure he wanted her to wear it again.

Then again, he was absolutely sure he wanted her out of it.

"Let me get you a towel," he said, stepping up on the patio and heading straight for a nearby cabinet where his mother always kept a neat stack. "Here, cover yourself and please be quick about it."

"Oh, I thought you liked my swimsuit," Tanya drawled, taking her time unfolding the oversize towel and draping it over her shoulders.

"I love it, which is why I don't want anyone else—mainly my brothers—to see you in it," Dev said, wrapping his own towel around his waist, tucking the ends in to keep it in place. "Or my body's reaction to you in it."

Tanya blushed, and he wanted to kiss her again.

And again.

"So what time are you picking me up for our date tonight…"

Dev's voice faded as a familiar *whop-whop* noise filled the air.

He immediately looked skyward, already knowing what he was searching for. His stomach took a nosedive, not stopping until it landed at his feet. Then, an arctic chill raced across his skin, raising goose bumps everywhere despite the warm temperatures.

"What is that?" Tanya asked.

Dev glanced at her; she was searching the skies, too. "It's a helicopter," he said, pointing as it moved in closer, becoming more defined just as his mother came out of the kitchen, drying her hands on a dish towel.

"I thought I heard… Oh!" Elise cried. "It's them! I wonder if your dad or Liam— Yes, there they are!"

She waved and the men acknowledged her with waves of their own from the other end of the yard nearer to the lake.

"Looks like the gang's all here," Dev muttered. "Adam, Fay and A.J. are heading this way from the parking lot."

They, too, had stopped and joined everyone else in looking upward.

Dev tracked the helo's progress, knowing his brother was at the controls. Determined not to allow the fear racing inside him to show on his face, he reached for his sunglasses but then realized he'd left them on top of the cabinet.

"Were you expecting this visit?" Tanya asked.

Dev nodded, but turned his face away from her and his

mother, keeping his gaze on the sky. "That's my brother, Bryant, in the family's new flying machine. His wife, Laurie, is riding shotgun."

The next moment he felt Tanya lace her fingers with his, giving them a quick squeeze. "Just think how close we were to being caught making out in the pool. By everyone and from every angle."

He smiled, appreciating her attempt to distract him, but seconds later when the helicopter dipped lower for a moment, Dev's breath vanished from his chest and he gripped her hand in his.

That's how it had started for him.

A sudden drop in altitude, a loss of pressure.

An easy fix. He was a trained pilot. He could handle the situation.

Yeah, right.

Tanya covered their joined hands with her other one, and he realized just how hard he'd been holding on to her.

For no reason.

It was easy to see that Bryant wasn't having any issues as he held the helicopter steady overhead for a moment before continuing on their way.

Dev eased his hold on Tanya as his family joined them poolside, Adam with a cell phone to his ear.

"It's Laurie," he said, speaking to everyone. "Everything is going great. They're heading back to the airstrip and should be here in less than an hour."

Dev untangled his hand from Tanya's and headed for the house, not looking at her or anyone else. "Excuse me. I'm going inside to change."

With every Murphy present on this beautiful May afternoon, except for the youngest brother, Ric, who was serving overseas in the Air Force, the backyard was crowded with kids and adults.

Alastair, the family patriarch, manned the grill with the precision of a general, having commandeered the barbecue tools from Nolan and Adam when they'd fought over how many times to flip the second round of hamburgers and hotdogs.

Elise sat nearby at the umbrella table with Laurie, Fay and Katie, who Tanya had quickly figured out was more like family than an employee to the Murphys. Abby sat with them, too, the teenager refusing to join the touch-football game between her brothers and her uncles, even though her dad promised he'd keep the twins from cheating.

Or accidently knocking her into the pool.

Still, Abby declined and Tanya couldn't blame her.

From where she stood at the far end of the deck near a table overloaded with food, the game seemed to be more about the guys tackling each other than any kind of organized sports activity.

At the moment, Bryant had one of his teenage nephews in some sort of makeshift choke hold as Liam casually stuck out his foot, sending Nolan, and the football he'd been carrying, toward the goal line that was marked by someone's sneakers, flying in two different directions. All the men started laughing.

Including Dev.

Standing nearby on the grass, dressed in cargo shorts and a faded blue T-shirt featuring the mascot of the Destiny High Blue Devils, Dev held his nephew, A.J., in his arms, having agreed to act as referee and makeshift babysitter.

Not that he'd really had any choice. There was no way he could've joined in on the roughhousing, but he didn't seem bothered by that as he laughed and traded verbal barbs with his brothers.

It was wonderful to see him so relaxed after witnessing the range of emotions that had crossed his face earlier today when Bryant had flown overheard in the family's helicopter.

Tanya had wanted to race after him when he'd disappeared inside the house, but instead had gone to use one of the guest bathrooms to shower and change, not surprised when Dev took almost an hour before joining them again.

He'd given her a quick nod when she'd asked if he was okay, making it clear he didn't want to talk about what had happened earlier.

"Boy, you've got it bad."

The plate full of freshly cut fruit Tanya was carrying almost slipped from her hand, but she flexed her still-aching fingers and held on to it. She turned to look at Mac. "What are you talking about?"

Mac gestured with his glass of iced tea.

"You'll have to be more specific than that, Mac."

"This…" Her grandfather kept his voice low as he again waved his glass in the air. "The big house, all the siblings, kids and grandkids. This is what you've always wanted."

Tanya stared at him. How did he know that?

"You used to live with me, remember? I wasn't a drunk all the time back then. On those days I was sober we would sit and watch old reruns of *The Waltons* while your mom was working. You always said you wanted what they had, lots of brothers and sisters, to be part of a big family."

Swallowing hard against the sudden lump in her throat, Tanya looked away. She couldn't believe he remembered those shared afternoons when she'd wanted to be one of those kids calling out goodnight to each other as the day ended. "I was an only child whose father had disappeared. Of course I wanted a family."

"And you got one. Eventually."

Yes, she did, but she and her mother had been on their own for many years by then, and with all the wisdom of a teenager, she'd believed she had long ago let go of her dream.

By the time her stepfather had come into the picture, and the twins followed not too long afterwards, Tanya had been a rebellious teen who'd often felt left out of the new life her mother had found for herself.

Thankfully, Tanya had been able to bridge the distance between her and her family years ago, but she had to admit there were times she still felt like an outsider when visiting them.

"You said something the other night about finding your destiny," Mac went on. "I thought you were talking about your upcoming trip, but maybe you meant it literally. As if what you've always been searching for is right here under your nose."

The lump in her throat had grown to the size of a volleyball and Tanya desperately needed a cold drink to wash it down. Grabbing her iced tea, she quickly gulped down half the glass.

Devlin Murphy—and his family—were not her destiny.

He was a mild distraction for the next few weeks.

Nothing more.

And if her heart said something different, then she would just wrestle it back into submission.

She was going to London, and that was that.

"Didn't your mama ever tell you it's impolite to stare? Even if the lady in question is quite stareable."

Dev blinked, grabbing baby A.J.'s chubby hand before

the kid slapped at his face again. He looked at Liam, annoyance racing through him at the sight of his brother's amused expression. "Is stareable even a word?"

Liam shrugged. "Who knows? It should be, because your lady is definitely stareable. You know, one who is easily stared at."

"Something you've been doing for the past ten minutes," Adam added, joining them and taking his son from Dev's arms. "Instead of watching my amazing touchdown pass to munchkin nephew number 1. But you saw your daddy's great arm, didn't you, pal?"

A.J. agreed by sending an all-out gum grin at his father.

"Hey, are we taking a break?" Nolan stepped up to the circle. "Please tell me we are. I'm getting too old for this stuff."

"Yes, we're taking a break." Dev leveled his gaze on Liam. "That goes for all of us."

Nolan waved off his sons, and the twins headed for the food.

"Who wants a drink?" Bryant asked, using the end of his T-shirt to wipe his sweaty face. "I'm buying."

All the brothers held up their hands, Dev included, wishing for a moment Bry would come back with five cold beers instead of four and whatever he grabbed for him.

Boy, he really wanted a drink right now.

No, scratch that.

He'd wanted a drink from the moment he'd seen the family's new bird appear over the backyard, and a nonalcoholic beverage just wasn't going to cut it.

From the looks he'd gotten from everyone from Tanya to his mother while they ate, he'd taken longer in the shower than normal. At least the pounding spray had drowned the clicking, whooshing and whining noises from a different helo that echoed inside his head.

Just when he'd thought he'd gotten rid of them, he was struck by the vision of his instrument panel dying—

"So, what are we talking about?" Nolan asked.

"Dev's girlfriend," Liam said.

Dev blinked, his brother's label pulling him back into their discussion. He realized too late that he had, in fact, been staring at Tanya.

What could he say?

She looked hot in a long white skirt that reached her ankles. A thin sliver of skin appeared between where her skirt met her hips and her colorful tank top, which looked as if his mother's fruit salad had exploded on it. Her hair was loose around her shoulders, and Dev's fingers itched to touch it again.

"Tanya is *not* my girlfriend."

"Okay, Dev's latest conquest."

He cuffed Liam on the back of the head. "She's not that, either."

"So, what is she?" Adam asked. "Other than your therapist?"

Dev stared at his brothers, wondering how this had suddenly turned into a conversation about him.

"She's a…friend," he finally said.

"A friendly friend if the action in the pool earlier today is any indication." Liam quickly stepped out of reach when Dev turned to him, his smirk still firmly in place.

"You saw that?" Dev asked.

"Right out my bedroom window. Not in detail, thanks to the distance between my place and the pool. You two were huddled in the corner, hidden from the house—good move to keep away from Mom's eagle eye, by the way—in the hot tub. Not hard to put two and two together."

"And you'd come up with five," Bryant said, returning with four chilled beers and one iced bottle of root beer.

He handed them out, adding, "That's why I'm the numbers man around here."

"No, I'd say more like fifteen to twenty." Liam grinned and twisted off the cap. "Yeah, I'd say at least twenty minutes of good old-fashioned making out."

"You watched them?" Nolan asked.

"You timed them?" Adam added.

"Watched who do what?" Bryant ignored his wife, who was calling to him from the deck. "What'd I miss?"

"Dev putting the moves on the next Murphy bride," Liam said, gesturing at his throat in a choking motion. "Another bachelor bites the dust."

Okay, it was time to turn this around and fast before Tanya got wind of their conversation. One good thing about having this many siblings was that there was always someone else with enough history to take the heat.

Dev knocked his soda bottle against Liam's beer. The glass-to-glass clinking noise was familiar, but somehow it just wasn't the same. "Shouldn't you be the next one to marry and start helping the folks with their never-ending need for grandchildren to spoil?"

"Why me? You're older."

"But you've got more experience," Dev shot back, knowing Liam couldn't dispute that fact.

"True, but with two failed marriages and no kids, I'm perfectly happy to play the favorite uncle and leave the parenting to you all."

"Two marriages and one love of your life if I remember correctly. What was that girl's name again?"

"What girl?" Adam and Nolan asked in unison.

"The one Liam was hanging around with that summer he just about gave the folks a heart attack by taking a pass on college to do the rodeo circuit," Dev said. "You know, that foreign chick who sounded like those British shows Mom is always watching on public television."

Bryant snapped his fingers. "Oh, right, I remember her. Blond, really pretty. Mattie or Margie or—"

"Missy," Liam cut him off. "Her name was Missy and she wasn't—isn't the love of my life."

"How come I don't remember this Missy?" Nolan asked.

"You were in Paris, brushing up on your architectural skills and meeting your own Murphy bride," Bryant said, waving at his wife when she called him again, "and Adam was off doing something with the Air Force Reserves that summer."

The brothers started walking toward the back deck, talking over each other as the conversation turned to Liam's checkered romantic history—both his marriages had lasted less than a year.

Mission accomplished, Dev thought with a grin.

"You're falling for her."

That came from Adam, who had hung back to walk next to him while doing his best to keep his infant son from gumming the lip of his beer bottle. Dev reached for it, giving his brother a sharp look when Adam's fingers tightened for a moment before he allowed him to tug it free.

Geez, did Adam really think he was going to chug half a warmish beer right here in front of everyone?

"No one has fallen for anyone. I've only kissed her twice, and we're going out on our first date tonight," Dev said, knowing Adam was waiting for him to say something. "We've only known each other three weeks."

"Not counting that one night ten years ago."

Yeah, not counting that.

"Hey, I knew Fay was the one for me back in high

school, and it took us over twenty years to get together. Don't make that mistake, bro."

"You're forgetting something, aren't you?" Dev kept his voice low but Tanya turned to look at him anyway, as if she knew he'd been talking about her. "She's leaving town in less than six weeks."

Chapter Twelve

"Oh, this place is so beautiful." Tanya leaned back against the faded patchwork quilt and propped herself up on her elbows. Stretching out her legs, she crossed her feet at the ankles, glad she'd pulled on her old cowboy boots. "I feel like I'm sitting on top of the whole world."

"Not the whole world," Dev said, then smiled as he continued to pack away the remains of their afternoon picnic. "My world, maybe."

After spending the last week pretty much immersed in his world, Tanya was finding she liked it here, really liked it, even if Mac's observations at last Saturday's barbecue had her moments away from canceling their plans for the drive-in movies that same night.

But then Dev had broken away from a discussion with his brothers to corner her in the empty kitchen, wanting to know what time he should pick her up for their date and stealing a heated kiss.

They'd had a good time that night, even though Dev concluded that drive-ins and his Jeep's bucket seats weren't a good match. He'd made up for that oversight once he'd got her back to the cabin.

Her first instinct had been to invite him inside, but it felt too soon, especially when Dev had never mentioned coming in, either. But then he'd driven past the soft glow of her cabin's front porch and parked on the far side of the building in the dark.

They'd sat in his Jeep, her on his lap, making out like teenagers for an hour before he'd walked her to her front door and said good night.

More dates followed this past week, and she'd attended his three physical therapy sessions in Laramie while continuing their daily pool sessions at his house.

They'd also had dinner with Mac at his place, gone to the weekly bingo night again, where he and Zip had shared the duties of master of ceremonies, and last night had had dinner at the Blue Creek Saloon, staying to dance to the music of a local band afterward. They were joined by his brothers Adam and Nolan and their wives.

But this afternoon's picnic here in the mountains outside Destiny had been a last-minute surprise of Dev's, and he'd insisted on taking on the responsibility for everything, from the food to the location to the cleanup.

Admitting his mother had helped a bit, he'd packed a terrific lunch of chicken pasta salad, a loaf of crusty bread and some of Elise's freshly baked brownies for dessert. He'd added an old blanket and a bottle of sparkling cider before they'd made a quick stop at her cabin so she could change from her casual yoga wear to jeans.

Then he'd taken the back roads, explaining that they were on the northern outskirts of Destiny as the blacktop gave way to dirt when they reached the foothills of the Laramie Mountains. He'd continued driving farther into the forest and higher on the mountain until they'd reached this spot.

It was a bit cooler up here, but they were in a clearing, surrounded by tall pines and blue spruces that stood far enough back to allow for plenty of sunshine and a pale blue sky. Dev had pointed out two ranches to the south of them, the Crescent Moon and the Triple G, both barely visible to the naked eye. They could see the faint outline of Destiny even farther beyond that.

As they'd gotten busy setting up the picnic, Tanya had found herself starting to wonder whether Dev had brought any other women up here before, until he'd told her this was a private place he came to often to get away from everything and enjoy the silence.

And it was his first time back since his accident.

They'd enjoyed their meal, talked about the progress Dev was making with another week of hard work under his belt, the firefighting crew training sessions and all the fantastic places Tanya wanted to visit while in the United Kingdom.

It was hard to believe the town would be celebrating Memorial Day on Monday and in another month she'd be leaving this quiet little ranching community for the busy streets of London at the end of next month.

Leaving Dev.

"I can totally understand why you come up here alone," she said, suddenly needing to break the awkward silence that had fallen over them as he packed the food away. "What a wonderful place to meditate and spend time alone with your thoughts."

He joined her on the blanket, mirroring her pose, only his legs extended a good foot past the quilt's edge. "Oh, is that the official woo-woo description of what I do here? I thought I was just enjoying the scenery and a little alone time."

She glared at him, going for her most evil scowl, but his grin was too infectious not to return. Then he closed his eyes, angling his Stetson down over his forehead to block the sun.

Watching the ease with which he moved—he no longer needed the cane—was so different from watching the man she'd met a month ago. His official test results that he'd shared with her said the same thing.

His recovery was speeding along now that he'd become fully committed to his sessions. He wasn't anywhere near being ready to get back to volunteer firefighting, but Tanya could see how much he missed it when he'd shared with her details of the training sessions for the competition next month.

She glanced down at where his hand lay so close to hers on the blanket. The need to touch him, to feel the connection they shared, was suddenly overwhelming, especially out here in the wide-open space that was the Wyoming wilderness.

As if he'd read her mind, Dev reached over and laced her fingers with his, without bothering to look at her or move any other part of his body.

"Does it bother you?" she asked, wondering if this area was like where his crash had happened. They'd talked about his accident a few times, but never at length. "Being in the forest like this after your accident and being lost for a couple of days last year?"

He shook his head, the Stetson gently rocking back and forth. "No. I've wanted to come back up to this place for a while now and I wanted to share it with you."

His words warmed her and she started to speak, but Dev kept on going.

"The place we went down was really dense. Nothing but trees for miles. I would've given my soul to find a wide-open space like this to try to land that bird. I tried to find…somewhere, but we were going in so fast. I did my best—"

A beeping noise filled the air. Dev swore under his breath.

"What is that?" Tanya asked.

"My cell phone."

"You get service way up here?"

He untangled their hands and sat up, righting his hat and digging into his back pocket at the same time. "Farther down the mountain, once you're in the foothills, it turns into a dead zone again until you hit the flatlands and are closer to town, but up here, yeah, they can find you." He thumbed the screen, surprise registering on his face. He hit a button and put the phone to his ear. "Hey, Chief. What's up?"

Tanya started to rise to give him some privacy as he spoke with his boss, but he tightened his grip on her, signaling it was okay for her to stay.

"No, I hadn't heard about any fire. Was it bad?" Dev stayed silent, but Tanya saw his expression go from curious to uneasy. "Well, that's good, but what does that have to do with—"

He went quiet again, listening. "Yes, that makes sense, but I wasn't planning—" His jaw clamped shut, a muscle ticking along the edge. "Yes, sir. Yes, it's a good thing the fairgrounds didn't dismantle the tower while prepping for the events on Monday. Okay, see you next week, Chief."

Dev ended the call and released his hold on her at the same time. Getting to his feet, he shoved his phone into his pocket and walked away a few feet, his back to her as he looked out over the expanse of land.

She didn't have any idea what was going on, so she sat and waited.

After a few minutes, he turned and started to pace in front of the blanket. "That was the fire chief."

"I figured that."

"The firefighting competition has to be moved from Johnson City due to a fire last night at their fairgrounds."

Not sure why that news would upset Dev so much, other than maybe his team had responded to the fire while they'd been dancing at the local bar, she remained silent.

"Destiny is going to be the new location. Well, the event took place here last year, too."

He glanced at her and she could read by his expression he wasn't happy about that. She played back his side of the conversation in her head, then said, "You're upset about the change in location because you weren't planning on going?"

He continued to stride back and forth, his silence giving her the answer she needed.

He hadn't planned on attending the event.

"But you've been working so hard with your crew. Why wouldn't you want to see them in action?"

"I know I'm being a complete idiot." Dev sighed, but kept moving. "Agreeing to help out, which I really had no choice in, thanks to the chief's persuasive methods, is one thing. Actually being there, watching them go all-out for the best time, to break records—" he jabbed at his chest with his thumb "—my record, when I can't even be an official member, can't do anything...when I...can't..."

His voice faded and Tanya could almost see the wheels turning in his head, but she had no idea what he was thinking.

He stopped, his gaze locked on something in the distance. Then he spun around, came back to the blanket and dropped to one knee in front of her. "I've changed my mind."

"About going to the competition?" She'd hoped so as she'd been looking forward to attending the event.

With him.

"About working with you. No more restrictions. Whatever you want me to do to get back to one hundred percent, I'm in. I know I'm almost there now, so I'm open to anything, from those crazy milkshakes to you cross-stitching 'Mama knows best' on my back with your miniature needles." He smiled, all charm and confidence. "We've still got a month, and starting first thing tomorrow—"

"Wait! Hold on a minute!" Tanya cut him off with a wave of her hand. She scooted backward, then struggled to get to her feet, Dev's rapid-fire words reverberating in her ears, throwing her off balance. "Please do not tell me you're actually thinking of participating. Are you crazy?"

Ohmigod, it was Tony all over again!

Tony Blackwell had been a brilliant skier, who had come out of nowhere a year ago and surprised the skiing community by winning three events on the World Cup Circuit at the tender age of fifteen.

An off-season training accident last summer had brought the teenager and his parents to the famed Crane Clinic where Tanya worked, looking for a miracle to get him back on the slopes.

A miracle worker she wasn't.

Not that he, his parents or the esteemed Dr. Ross Crane—her former boss and lover—would accept that.

Or her assessment and final decision when it came time for Tony to rejoin his team.

Nausea filled her and her heart pounded hard in her chest. She forced away the past and concentrated on the madness happening right now.

"You can't do that. You cannot compete."

Dev shot to his feet. "I was only thinking about—"

"You told me those challenges are replicas of what a firefighter is expected to be able to do on a daily basis, whenever he or she responds to a call." She cut him off. "Isn't that right?"

He nodded. "Yes, that's true."

"You have made a remarkable recovery, Dev." Tanya latched on to his arm, her grip tight, needing him to look at her, to understand what she was saying. "A recovery you've earned from all your hard work, but as I've told you from the beginning, this is still a recovery that's ongoing. It's way too soon for you to consider doing that kind of physically demanding activity, even if it's just a friendly competition."

"Okay, I hear what you're saying."

"Do you really?" His expression was conciliatory at best, and the idea of Dev doing something that could cause serious damage—permanent damage—to his body, all in the name of a sport, made her physically ill. "Do you understand I'm speaking here not as some girl you've been trying to charm into your bed, but as a professional?"

Dev peeled her fingers from his arm, then took both of her shaking and clammy hands in his. "Yes, I hear you, but, honey, what's going on? You are as pale as a ghost and shaking like a newborn foal."

He was right—she was acting irrational.

Closing her eyes, Tanya forced deep, slow breaths in through her nose and pushed the air past her lips. One, two, three times. "I'm sorry, I— Oh, I honestly didn't see this coming. I shouldn't have reacted that way. I feel... so stupid."

"You're not stupid, you're upset."

Dev held tight when she tried to pull from his touch,

and when he moved closer, bringing her into his arms, she found herself going willingly. The strength of his embrace and the steady beat of his heart beneath her cheek calmed her. "Do you want to tell me what just happened here?"

She wasn't sure she did, but the man deserved an explanation. She just didn't think she could get the words out at this moment. "Not…not right now, okay?"

"Sure." He kissed her forehead, his hands gently moving over her back. "Whenever you're ready to talk, I'm here to listen."

A half hour later, their picnic officially over, Dev steered his Jeep back down the mountain. He glanced over every now and then at Tanya sitting quietly in the passenger seat.

She still hadn't told him what had caused her outburst back on the summit, but he suspected it had to do with something much bigger than his new ideas about his therapy regimen.

He'd actually considered for a moment the possibility that if he went all out with his workouts from now on, including agreeing to one of her dreaded acupuncture sessions, there might be an off chance he could compete in one of the less strenuous events next month.

Not the smartest plan, he conceded, but the chief's call had thrown him for a loop because he really hadn't planned on attending the annual competition.

In fact, he'd been entertaining the idea of stealing Tanya away that same weekend to a luxury resort somewhere, seeing how she was scheduled to leave for London the Tuesday following the competition.

He'd first thought about Reno, but that would mean flying.

Dev loosened his grip on the steering wheel, flexing

his fingers and forcing himself to relax. He wasn't ready to even think about getting back in the air again, but he had to admit Tanya asking about the crash had made him think.

Maybe it was time to read the official report for himself. It had been sitting on the corner of his desk for the last week after he'd asked Katie to make him a copy.

Right around the time he'd asked her to make sure all the paperwork was in place so he could fly to and represent the family business in the United Kingdom.

Just in case.

"Dev, what is that? Up there in the road?"

Tanya's words, the first she'd spoken since they started back down the mountain, had him looking at her and then to where she pointed.

He slowed the Jeep to a crawl, realizing a small figure was frantically waving, trying to get their attention. As they got closer, he saw it was young girl, her blond hair in long braids, who raced to them when he stopped.

"Boy, I'm glad to see you!" She brushed at her dirty face, but the evidence that she'd been crying was still on her cheeks. "We need help!"

Dev easily placed the girl, considering their proximity to the Crescent Moon Ranch. "You're Landon and Maggie Cartwright's girl, aren't you? What are you doing way out here?"

She nodded, sending her braids flying. "Yes, I'm Anna Cartwright. Jacoby Dillon and I were hiking up the road and he fell in a hole. Please help him!"

Dev reached for the girl and helped her climb over the side and into the vehicle's backseat. He made a left turn onto the dirt path, following where she pointed while Tanya insisted the girl put on her seatbelt.

They drove through the trees for a few minutes before Anna wanted them to stop. This was the place.

Dev parked the Jeep, tossed his hat into the backseat and grabbed his flashlight. Maggie's daughter scrambled out of the backseat right behind him. "Tanya, can you get the rope and first-aid kit from the storage area in the back? I'm going ahead with Anna."

Tanya nodded and Dev followed the little girl, his gaze already latched on to the gaping three-foot-wide crevasse a few yards ahead. "Hang on, Anna. I don't want you anywhere near that. We don't need both of you in trouble."

"He's down there." Anna skidded to a stop in the dirt and rocks. "Jacoby! I'm back! Can you hear me? I've got the bingo guy and his girlfriend with me!"

Dev crouched beside the opening. "Hey, Jacoby, my name is Devlin Murphy and I'm a member of the Destiny Volunteer Fire Department."

A faint response came up from the dark shadows of the hole.

He directed Anna to a nearby rock, glad when the girl obeyed his hand signal. The ground was soft and loose beneath his feet. Not a good sign, but at least the boy seemed to be able to communicate.

Dev inched closer, needing to figure out what kind of situation they had here. "You doing okay?"

"I think so, sir," came the reply from down in the earth. "My ankle and my shoulder hurt real bad."

"Are you standing up? Can you move around?"

"Yes, sir. I sort of slid down the side, but I'm standing now. There's a stream of sunlight directly overhead, but otherwise it's pretty dark down here."

And scary as hell, Dev thought, but the fact the boy could see sunlight and carry on a conversation with them hopefully meant he wasn't that far down. "Don't worry, Jacoby. We're going to get you out."

Tanya arrived with the stuff he'd asked for, along with the quilt and the cider. She tended to Anna while Dev reached for his cell phone, even though he knew exactly where they were.

Just as he thought. No service. *Damn!*

"Okay, here's what we're going to do." He spoke loud enough so the boy could hear his plan. "Jacoby, I've got a hundred feet of rope. I'm going to make a lasso at one end and lower it down to you. I need you to slip it over your head, down around your chest and then pull it tight under your arms so we can lift you out of there."

"Yes, sir."

"How old are you, Jacoby?"

"Nine, sir."

"So you weigh about fifty-five or sixty pounds?"

"We just had our physicals for baseball and I'm almost seventy. I'm big for my age."

The boy sounded proud, and he had every right to be considering the condition he'd been in when he'd come to town a few years ago. Justin Dillon had certainly turned his son's life around once he'd found out the boy existed.

Still, the kid's weight wasn't going to make this any easier. This time last year, it would've been no problem for him to haul up that much, but now? Dev wasn't sure he and Tanya could do this together, but they had to try.

Then he had an idea.

Tanya hurried to him when he waved at her. "My keys are still in the Jeep. Back it up to us, okay? But don't come any closer than that rock where the girl is."

"Why? What are you planning?"

"I'm going to use the Jeep's towing hitch to create an improvised pulley system. Once we get the boy secure,

I'll feed the line while you slowly drive forward, and we'll pull him out of there."

Dev read concern in Tanya's eyes, but she turned away and headed for his Jeep. He then explained his idea to the two kids while creating the lasso. Minutes later, Tanya arrived, stopping when Dev signaled.

"Anna why don't you go sit with Tanya? You'll need to be her eyes as she drives forward because she'll be watching for my signals."

The girl nodded and raced for the vehicle. Dev looked at Tanya, knowing she understood that he didn't want the girl to watch this, just in case something went wrong.

"Okay, we're ready to put this plan into action, Jacoby." Dev moved as close to the hole as he dared, then tossed the lasso down inside. He prayed the earth around the ragged edge of the opening would hold up against the pressure. "Here comes the lasso. Do you see it?"

"I see it."

Dev slowly fed the rope down into the hole. "Give a tug when you have it in your hands." The jerk came seconds later. "Now, do as I instructed and make sure you slide the slipknot as tight as you can around your chest."

"Yes, sir."

The rope moved in Dev's grip. He tried to picture the kid doing as he'd asked when a sharp cry rose out from the hole. He wanted to race over there and see for himself what was going on, but the ground was so unstable.

"Hey, buddy, you all right?" Dev called out.

"No, it's my shoulder. I can't lift it." The boy's voice faltered. "I can't move it."

Meaning it was probably dislocated.

"I'm sorry, but it hurts too much."

"That's okay, Jacoby. Don't worry. I've got another idea." Dev waved at the Jeep, getting Tanya's attention.

She turned off the vehicle, said something to Anna—probably telling her to stay put—and then raced to him.

"Jacoby's hurt. Probably dislocated his shoulder. He can't get the rope tied securely around himself," Dev quickly explained to her while trying his cell phone again. Still nothing. They were going to need more help and they had to either get to the Cartwrights' or within cell phone range. "You and Anna take my Jeep and head the rest of the way down the mountain. Keep trying your phone until you can get through. I'm going to stay here with Jacoby until you get back."

"Mr. Murphy!" The kid's voice called out, now with an edge of panic to it. "There's water down here now."

Tanya's eyes grew wide. "What does that mean?" she whispered.

Dev could guess, but he didn't like the answer. "How much?"

"I'm standing in a puddle that wasn't here a few minutes ago. My sneakers are soaked."

Dammit! "Is there anything solid down there you can climb on or stand on?"

"I don't think so."

There was only one solution. "Jacoby, I need for you to let go of the rope, okay?"

"You're not leaving me, are you?"

Dev's heart went out to the kid as the line went slack. "Of course not. My friend Tanya and Anna are going to get help, but I'm staying right here with you." He looked around and spotted the closest tree that was sturdy enough for the job. "In fact, I'm coming down there to wait with you."

"You're what?" Tanya whispered, following him as he headed for the tree. "Are you crazy?"

"That's something we don't have time to debate at the

moment." Dev wrapped the end of the rope around the tree, securing it, but leaving plenty of length for him to use. "You need to get going."

"Dev, I can't leave when you're about to do something—"

"What I'm about to do is my job, Tanya."

He turned to face her, seeing that same panic in her eyes as earlier when she'd lectured him about the competition. "This isn't a game or about showing off. There's a kid in a bad situation that's getting worse by the minute and it's my job to rescue him or keep him safe until enough help arrives to make that happen." He reached out and cupped her cheek. "This is who I am. This is what I do. Can you try to understand that?"

Tears filled her eyes, but she nodded.

"Now go. Give your phone to Anna so she can keep trying to reach someone while you drive. Take the blanket with you, and when you get back out to the main road, lay it flat with some rocks to keep it in place."

"As a place maker for where you are. Got it." Wrapping her hand around his neck, she pulled him down for a quick kiss. "But I'm not leaving until I know you two are okay down there."

Knowing it was useless to argue, Dev grabbed the rope and headed back for the hole. He emptied what he could of the first-aid kit into his pockets, tucked the flashlight into the waistband of his jeans and then lay flat on the ground, distributing his weight as evenly as possible.

"Jacoby, I'm crawling toward the edge of the hole. Then I'm going to swing down inside. Move as close to one side as you can and keep your head down."

"Yes, sir."

Dev inched forward until he reached the edge. From the looks of it, the hole was about thirty feet deep. Roots and sticks jutted out from the walls, but nothing substantial that would assist with climbing down.

Nope, this was going to be all on him.

He looked back over his shoulder and found Tanya standing a safe distance away. "Approximately thirty feet deep, three feet wide."

She nodded.

He focused his attention back on the crevasse and saw the boy pressed against one wall in the shadows. "I'm coming in, Jacoby. I'll be right there. Keep your head down until I tell you otherwise."

The tiny head bobbed. Dev swung his body around and went in feet first, using his upper body strength to hold himself steady as he slowly moved, hand over hand, deeper into the crater.

At the last moment he glanced up and saw Tanya watching him.

"Go," he said.

She mouthed something in return, but he couldn't be sure if she'd asked him to be careful or just said she loved him.

Chapter Thirteen

By the time the Destiny Fire Department arrived, the water level was waist high on Devlin.

Once he'd gotten safely to the bottom of the hole, he'd used his T-shirt to create a splint for Jacoby's shoulder. Then he'd done what he could to patch up some scratches on the kid's hands and face. Handing over the flashlight for him to hold, Dev had hoisted the boy into his arms, trying to keep him as dry as possible.

The water must have come from an underground spring because it was freezing cold. Bad enough when it soaked through his jeans and filled his boots, but when it came in direct contact with his skin, Dev had hissed. It had felt like a million tiny toothpicks jabbing him.

Or needles.

Yeah, he'd been second-guessing his decision about allowing Tanya to play stick-the-needle wherever she wanted on his body long before they came across the two kids needing their help.

Long before his mind must've played tricks on his heart.

She loved him?

No, there was no way that was what she'd said just before he'd slipped into the hole.

Pushing that thought out of his head had been easy because after he'd done all he could for Jacoby, they'd chatted about baseball and comic books, anything to keep the kid's mind off their situation.

And the rising water.

By the time it reached Dev's backside, he'd handed over his cell phone to the kid, checking the time and noting that almost twenty minutes had passed since they'd heard the honking of the Jeep's horn as Tanya had driven away.

He'd been busy trying to calculate how much longer they had before he really needed to worry about the rising water, figuring Jacoby could sit on his shoulders if it came to that when the sounds of galloping horses told them someone had arrived.

The kid had gotten upset when he'd first heard his dad's voice, but then he calmed down when his father reassured him he wasn't angry. It turned out Justin Dillon and Landon Cartwright had been out looking for the kids when they came across Tanya and Anna. After they'd exchanged information, the men had sent the girls farther down the hill to continue their search for a cell phone signal, and they'd ridden away to find the crevasse.

Dev, Landon and Justin had been debating how to create a sling for Jacoby—or if they should even attempt hoisting him out—for a good half hour when the decision was taken out of their hands.

Tanya had returned, the sheriff and the fire department only minutes behind her.

Things had moved quickly then, with the civilians pushed back and the professionals taking over.

"We've just about got the tripod rigging secure up here." The chief's booming voice easily carried over the noise from above. "You two doing okay?"

"Roger that," Dev called up, shielding his eyes.

He figured he and the kid had been down here for over an hour now. It was still light outside, but the sun had moved, so they needed an electrical spotlight to see in the hole.

Thankfully, the water hadn't risen any higher than Dev's belly button. "But I went numb from the waist down a while ago."

"Funny, I always figured you for numb from the neck up." Zip stuck his head into the opening, grinning at them. "How's the shoulder holding out, Jacoby?"

"It's numb, too, but I'm okay," the boy said, looking up, the protective helmet they'd lowered for him slipping off the back of his head. "Tell my dad I've changed my mind about playing baseball when I grow up. I want to be a firefighter. Like Mr. Dev."

"You hear that, Zippenella?" The kid's words warmed his heart, even though he wasn't a firefighter—volunteer or otherwise—anymore.

"Yeah, I heard. Kid, we gotta talk about role models once we get your butt out of there."

Dev was about to tell Zip where he could stick his role model when the man backed away from the edge under the chief's orders. Things moved quickly then as the team got into place and the motorized pulley lowered a sling into the hole.

It took a few moments to get Jacoby into the contraption, and Dev admired how he never said a word even though his arm had to be killing him. Dev held on to the boy as long as he could, raising his hands over his head, silently cursing a blue streak at the pain racing through his shoulders.

A cheer went up when Jacoby was captured in a fire-fighter's arms.

Dev dropped his hands, splashing at the water gathered around his hips. Now that Jacoby was safe, he tried to move his feet, but his boots had sunk into the mud and muck beneath him.

"Hey, Murphy, you're next. Heads up."

Reaching out, he grabbed the sling as it was lowered again, this one a much bigger size. He still had to extend the straps as far as he could before slipping it over his head and shoulders. Securing it tightly beneath his arms, he signaled he was ready.

"I'm at least ankle deep in the mud down here so this could take a few minutes," he said, warning the crew.

"Get ready. We've lifting you now."

Dev braced himself and tried to stay relaxed at the same time. The motor above roared to life again and for a moment it was machine versus mud, but finally the machine won and Dev's feet slipped free of his boots as he was slowly lifted out of the hole.

"Welcome back, cowboy." Zip smiled at him and held out his hand.

The air was fresh and sweet across his skin as Dev latched on to his buddy's hand, using the leverage to swing himself over to solid ground.

Which didn't feel too solid beneath his wet stocking feet at the moment.

The crew got him out of the sling in record time, and everyone except those working now to dismantle the heavy duty rigging moved away from the danger. A blanket was placed over Dev's shoulders as Zip and another firefighter directed him toward the rescue truck, where he could see Jacoby was getting looked over, his father, Justin, right there with him. Anna and Landon Cartwright were right by their side, too.

Where was Tanya?

Dev looked around, finally spotting her on the outskirts of all the craziness, standing next to the driver's side of his Jeep. She stared at him with one arm crossed over her middle, a hand pressed to her mouth as if she was holding back calling his name.

He wanted to wave, to let her know he was okay, but his arms felt like lead weights after holding Jacoby for so long.

The desire to go to her, to feel the heat of her body against his, almost dropped him to his knees. Settling for a smile and wink that he hoped she could see, Dev then headed for the EMTs, knowing he wouldn't be allowed to leave without at least getting a preliminary check, despite the fact he didn't have a scratch on him.

Ten minutes later, cell phone back in hand and his wet jeans stuck to his lower half like glue, Dev got the all clear to leave. He accepted Jacoby and Justin's thanks, gave the same to the chief and the crew for everything they did and then headed straight for Tanya.

Everything would be okay once he got her in his arms again.

As he got closer, he could see a mixture of relief and fear in her eyes. "I'm good. We both are. Jacoby is heading into town to get checked out for a dislocated shoulder at the clinic, but other than that, the loss of my handmade boots to Middle Earth and needing a hot shower, everything is good."

She exhaled and closed her eyes, reaching out to lay a hand on the blanket he still had wrapped around him. "I was so…worried."

Her other hand joined the first, her fingers curling into the blanket. Ignoring how his muscles screamed at the movement, Dev wrapped his arms around her, pulling her to his chest.

Damn, he hurt everywhere.

In a way he hadn't since his first physical therapy session back when the casts were removed three months ago, but he wasn't going to tell her that.

"I'd like to get out of here. Do you mind driving?" he asked.

Tanya let go of the blanket and stepped back. He already missed her warmth. "I'll take you anywhere you want to go."

He liked the sound of that.

Walking around to the passenger side of the Jeep and not falling flat on his face or showing his total discomfort took just about all of his strength. What little he had left was used up crawling into the Jeep. Tanya got behind the wheel and they headed back toward town.

As soon as he got a signal, Dev called the house, thankful when his father answered the phone. The chief had said he'd notified his family about what was going on, but had told them to stay away from the accident site. Dev quickly explained everything that had happened and reassured his dad he was okay.

Tanya drove through the center of town and headed toward the Murphy homestead, but when she put on the blinker to turn down the main road, Dev waved her off and ended the call.

"I thought you'd want to go home," she said, taking her eyes off the road for a moment to look at him.

"I want to be with you."

His words hung in the air between them. Tanya only

looked at him for a moment longer, then put her gaze back on the road ahead.

When the Jeep slowed, Dev honestly didn't know if she was going to turn the thing around and take him back to his place or not. Then she put the blinker on again but made the left turn that took them toward Mac's farm.

Minutes later, she pulled to a stop in front of the cabin and shut the engine off. He was out of the passenger's side and on the porch by the time she joined him there. Tanya stepped aside to let him enter first. Dev waited until she closed the door behind her before hauling her into his arms.

The blanket floated to the floor at their feet as he backed her up against the closest wall and devoured her mouth in a kiss that was frantic, primal and passionate.

It was the way he'd wanted to kiss her up on the mountain. The way he'd wanted to kiss her the moment he'd crawled out of that hole and found her waiting for him.

And she kissed him back.

She was right here with him, matching his desire, his need with her own. Her hands clutched at his shoulders, bringing their bodies even closer together. Then she grabbed his neck as she moaned against his mouth, the moist heat of her lips sending shivers throughout his body.

Shivers that turned to tremors, tremors he couldn't control as his entire body shook with the power she had over him.

"Dev…" She dragged her mouth from his. "Dev, you're shaking."

"I—I know." Geez, even his words were unsteady. "See what y-you do to m-me."

"I think this is more of a delayed reaction to the rescue than to me." She pushed against his chest and his hands fell away, releasing her. "You need to get out of those wet clothes and into a hot shower. Don't move. I'll be right back."

Yeah, that wouldn't be a problem. He wasn't going anywhere.

Despite how he'd kissed her seconds ago, it was as if every muscle in his body was on lockdown. Unable to move, but afraid he would end up on the floor, he braced his hands, and then his forehead, against the wall.

She slipped away.

Closing his eyes, he listened while she moved around the cabin. The light changed behind his eyelids; she must have closed the blinds. A few minutes later, a musky, spicy fragrance filled his nose. Candles. Then the soft strains of music reached his ears, something easygoing and instrumental filling the air before the steady pulsating sound of the shower in the nearby bathroom almost drowned it out.

Damn, that was the best sound of all, but he wasn't sure he could walk the few feet necessary to get there.

He flexed his fingers. Okay, that was a start.

Palms flat, he pushed, straightening his arms. A low, guttural moan fell from his lips before he could swallow it back and he prayed Tanya hadn't heard that pathetic sound.

But she probably had. She was right there next to him. He could feel her.

"The shower is ready when you are."

He was ready. Boy, was he ready.

Opening his eyes, Dev stared at the plank wall while mentally gathering the last ounce of strength he had. He stepped back, turned and headed for the bathroom on the far side of the cabin.

Tanya was there reaching for him, but he held up a hand and kept moving. He could do this on his own. Ten steps. Fifteen, tops. Then the hot steam enveloped him, seeping into his skin.

He reached for the button fly of his jeans and stripped them and his briefs away in one motion. The socks took a couple attempts, but soon they were gone, too.

Pulling open the glass door, he stepped inside. This time his moan was one of pure appreciation as the hot spray covered his body. He ducked his head under the water and let it pound against his neck and shoulders. Already the muscles were loosening and coming back to life.

Damn, that felt good.

Almost as good as having Tanya in his arms.

Tanya…

Raising his head from out of the spray, he brushed the water from his face and found her standing right outside the shower, holding the glass door open.

Staring at him.

His body responded to the appreciation in her gaze.

"If you're feeling better, would you like some company?" she asked.

He read her lips more than heard the words. This time he was sure of what she'd said.

"Yes, please."

She released the door and it started to close, but Dev held it open, not wanting to miss one moment of her undressing.

Grabbing the bottom edge of her shirt, she pulled it over her head in a smooth motion. The ponytail she must've put into place sometime during the afternoon disappeared. Her hair once again floated like a soft cloud around her shoulders as she bent to remove her aged boots and then her socks. When she straightened, her fingers were already at her waist and the jeans were gone in a heartbeat.

She now stood there, dressed only in a white lacy bra, matching panties and a shy smile.

Yes, please.

In one motion, he reached for her.

Wrapping his arm around her waist, he pulled her under the water with him, the glass door closing with a soft thud, cocooning them in a private world that was theirs alone.

"Dev!" She called out his name, then laughed. "You're getting me wet!"

As he hauled her up against him, his arousal pressed into the softness of her belly. He filled his hands with the perfection that was her lace-covered bottom. "I want you wet."

Tanya's laughter melted into a moan as Dev's mouth slid from her jaw to her neck to her collarbone.

He kept moving until his mouth reached her breast, and he took the nipple between his lips, lace included. Tugging, licking, teasing. He did it all, paying attention to each action as his fingers drew the straps off her shoulders.

She thought about the front closure on her bra, but he found it and whisked the sodden material from her body. The panties soon followed and then his hands were everywhere.

Touching, caressing.

Her fingers followed the same path on his body. She wanted to explore every inch of his naked perfection, spurred by the desire he created in her and her own need to make sure he was truly okay after today's harrowing ordeal.

She knew he'd had to help that little boy, but she'd been so scared…

"It's okay," Dev whispered, his mouth at her ear. "I'm okay."

It was then Tanya realized she'd spoken her fears aloud.

Closing her eyes, she tipped her head back and let the shower wash away her tears.

Today had been the closest she'd ever come to this kind of emergency, and now she realized, in a small way, how terrifying this part of Dev's life was. His day job had him sitting at a desk most of the time, designing home security systems. Sometimes he supervised the installation at the construction site.

But firefighting?

That meant putting his life on the line, and not for entertainment or competition like the event coming up next month, but every time he answered the call of an alarm....

"It's just us, just you and me." His words filled the steamy air around them. "I want you...wanted to be with you from the moment I first saw you."

"I've wanted you, too."

Always.

Tanya bit hard on her bottom lip, managing to hold back that last word from being said aloud, but not able to hide the truth from herself any longer.

She'd fallen in love with this man.

This temporary distraction, a way to stay busy as she waited to close the door on her old life before starting over again, had taken root deep inside her heart without her even knowing it.

Moments later, Dev shut off the water, opened the shower door and wrapped her in one of the large, white fluffy towels hanging on the hook outside. He used the other towel for himself, his hands never leaving her body while his whispered words told her all he wanted to do.

To her. With her.

She had started out wanting to take care of him, but somehow he'd turned everything around as he backed her into the main room and headed straight for the bed.

"Are you okay to walk?" she asked as they stumbled over each other's feet. "You're not too tired?"

Dev smiled and said, "Right now, honey, I feel like I could fly."

Pushing the blankets to one side, he laid her down on the cool sheets, and then joined her. His mouth covered hers again as he gently freed her body from the damp towel, and soon she did the same to him.

"Please tell me you have a condom somewhere close by. My wallet is in the bathroom, still in the back pocket of my jeans."

She smiled up at him and pointed to the small bedside table on the far side of the bed.

Dev looked over his shoulder, and then lay back against the covers, reaching for the single drawer. Tanya used that moment to move across his body, getting there first.

His hands encircled her waist as she grabbed a couple of packets, tossing them on the pillow. "Hey, where do you think you're going?"

She straddled his hips, the hardness of him in perfect alignment with the wetness of her center. "Oh, right here seems perfect to me."

He groaned as she rocked against him, and then his mouth found her breasts again. Stroking, caressing, he built a fire within her until she was ready to explode.

She reached for him, but he grabbed her wrist. "No...I won't last. Been so long."

Sitting tall, she slid farther down his legs. Bracing her hands on her thighs, she watched as he sheathed himself, a thrill racing through her as his hands trembled. Once he was done, he motioned for her, and she went to him.

A ragged murmur came from his throat as she braced against his chest and slowly lowered herself, accepting him. He held her hips in place when she started to move, the two of them falling into a natural rhythm as if they'd done this many times before.

"So perfect," he whispered, looking up at her, watching her. "You are so perfect. This is so perfect…"

"For me," she finished his sentence, his thoughts matching her own. "Perfect for me."

The slow pulse deep inside grew, sensations rushing to every inch of her as he arched, lifting his hips off the bed to meet hers, his control spiraling away until he took her with him over the edge.

Dev tried to stay relaxed, pretending he was back on that lumpy mattress surrounded by the citrusy lavender scent that was uniquely Tanya's.

They'd spent an amazing night in her bed, making love again and again, except when they'd gotten up around midnight and made scrambled eggs. That's when they talked about what had made Tanya so upset during their picnic yesterday.

It was hard to listen to her story about her young patient, a skier whose name he recognized right away, but what had been worse was hearing how the kid and his parents had refused to listen to her professional advice.

They had every right to get a second opinion, even if that opinion came from Tanya's boss. But when they ignored Tanya's recommendation to take more time off from competing and the kid ended up suffering a career-ending injury, it had been Tanya who'd lost her job, thanks to that spineless loser she called a boyfriend, who'd caved under the pressure and fired her.

And then the jerk had actually threw the monetary favor he'd done for her back in her face.

Dev now understood two things—her aversion to accepting help and why she'd been upset about his off-the-cuff plan to get into the firefighting competition.

Without referencing anything to do with assistance or patronage, he assured her that he did value her opinion about his health and that he wouldn't take any unnecessary risks.

Thanks to a second shared shower, one that lasted much longer than the first, he'd shown her just how much better he was feeling.

That is, until he'd been awakened this morning by a killer cramp in his lower leg, the first one he'd had in weeks.

He hadn't even realized he'd cried out until Tanya's strong hands were on his body, working her magic. She'd gotten rid of the cramp and then proceeded to give him an all-over massage that had him falling back asleep without even realizing it.

Or remembering that he'd agreed to an acupuncture session.

"Are you sure about this?" Tanya walked out of the bathroom, drying her hands. "I know you mentioned doing this during the picnic, but that was before your unplanned rescue. I'm worried you've taken a step back in your recovery because of what happened yesterday."

He didn't want to say that he agreed with her, but yeah, he was hurting after what he put his body through rescuing Jacoby. "We're going to see Pete tomorrow, but I'd be more worried if I wasn't sore this morning. Besides, you're the one who promised great results from this pincushion stuff."

Geez, it was a good thing he was lying down.

Thankfully he was on his stomach. Not that he planned on watching her stick him, but this way there was no chance of him seeing the needles because Tanya had already mapped out the specific pressure points on his back.

"You ready?"

She laid a hand on his shoulder and damned if he didn't relax at her touch. "Ready when you are. Just keep talking, okay?"

Chapter Fourteen

Tanya perched the straw Stetson on her head. It came complete with two beautiful yellow silk roses positioned right next to the turquoise blue stones on the hat band.

She did a bit of posturing, looking at her reflection from all angles, but she'd known from the moment she'd spotted this beauty among the dozens of hats on display that this one was just what she'd been looking for.

"Oh, Dev, it's perfect." She whirled away from the mirror hanging on the side of the vendor's tent and forced herself to beam at the man standing behind her. "I love it."

Dev grinned at her and paid for the hat.

Tanya had arrived at the Destiny fairgrounds an hour ago with Mac, knowing Dev had been here since early morning with his team, getting ready for the day's events.

Her grandfather had disappeared in the crowd after they'd found Dev, but he planned to join her later on when the challenges started. They'd sit with Dev's family, some of whom she and Dev had already run into as they walked around the area roped off for vendors selling everything from food to balloons to hats.

"You're going to have to wear that on the plane so as not to crush it." Dev took her hand as they moved on, his words deflating her mood just a bit. "Hard to believe in a little over forty-eight hours you'll be winging your way to jolly ol' England."

Yes, sometimes Tanya found it hard to believe, too.

Especially since her flight left tomorrow night, not Tuesday as previously planned.

Unable to sleep, she'd crawled out of Dev's arms in the wee hours of the morning and through tears she couldn't hold back, logged on to the computer and changed her departure time. Not wanting to lose it in front of him and have a teary-eyed goodbye, she'd decided to make the break quick, so she could cry in private if she wanted to.

If she wanted to?

Crying was inevitable, because the past four wonderful weeks had flown by as she and Dev continued to spend just about every day, and most nights, together.

After taking it easy on the advice of his doctors for a few days following Jacoby Dillon's rescue, Dev had jumped back into his therapy program full force, both with Pete and with her.

Including at least two acupuncture sessions a week.

She'd been amazed at how well he'd handled the first session. So well that he'd actually fallen asleep during the resting period. He'd had nothing but praise for her skills when she woke him after it was over, insisting his pain was gone.

Tanya hadn't been sure if he was only telling her what he thought she wanted to hear, but when he'd come to her a few days later and asked to do it again, she agreed, and to his family's surprise, started to include the sessions in his therapy schedule.

Of course, it hadn't been all work between them.

They had plenty of time for movies, dinners out, weekly bingo nights, special events like the blessing ceremony for Adam and Fay's son in the family's beautiful log chapel and a road trip to Colorado Springs to see her family one more time.

Her mother and stepfather had liked him right away and he'd charmed her twin sisters, just as she knew he would. They spent a lot of time with Devlin's family, too, and Tanya had found herself falling in love with them as much as she was in love with Dev.

But she had no idea if he felt the same way about her.

They had fun together and their physical relationship was unlike any she'd ever had before, but both of them worked hard to keep things casual and easy and light.

Just like they'd said from the very beginning.

"I hate to do this, but I've got to run." Dev checked his watch. "The individual events are starting soon."

"And you need to be there for the team."

He'd told her a few days ago he'd been officially cleared as a member of the Destiny Fire Department challenge team, a requirement for him to be able to have access to the team's staging area and to be allowed on the competition grounds.

His name wasn't listed as a participant in any of the events, just as one of two backups each team was allowed in case injuries required a team member to be replaced.

"Go on." She waved him off, hoping her words sounded causal. "I'll be cheering for DFD from the stands."

He grabbed her around the waist and pulled her between two vendor tents, using the private space to kiss her so thoroughly and possessively that her breath disappeared.

"It might be the rest of the day before I can do that again," he whispered against her lips, his own breath coming out in short gasps, "so I wanted to make it worthwhile."

She closed her eyes, knowing the few hours they had tonight were going to be the last. How was she ever going to find the strength to say goodbye to this man?

Dev gave Tanya another quick kiss and then turned and walked away before he did something stupid.

Like tell her he loved her.

Keep things casual. Don't get in the way of her plans. Don't mess this up.

Dev had repeated those rules to himself over and over as one day melted into the next and Tanya slowly became ingrained in his life.

In his heart.

He'd kept his feelings to himself, not wanting to put a damper on the great times they were having, but a plan to surprise her in London was already underway.

Maybe in the fall when things slowed down around the office.

Pushing that idea to the back of his mind for now, Dev switched gears and concentrated on getting ready for today's competition.

He'd been over the moon to find out he'd passed the physical to make the team, even if it was just as a replacement member. The chances of him being needed to step in and fill a space during any of the team events were slim.

But he'd done it.

He'd made it back, thanks to the hard work of a lot of people, including Tanya.

Not telling her about taking the physical had felt wrong, but he didn't want to upset her, especially if he didn't pass. When he did, she'd been the first person he'd shared the news with, even before his teammates. He'd expected her to be upset, but she'd surprised him by congratulating him with a big hug and a kiss.

After making sure he wasn't actually competing.

"Hey, Murphy!" Zip called out to him from the area set aside for the Destiny Fire Department's team to stage their equipment and get ready for the individual challenges that were happening first. "Get your head out of the clouds! We start in less than an hour."

By the time the day's schedule allowed for a lunch break, Dev was dirty, sweaty and tired, but he felt great.

The Destiny team was kicking butt all over the place and he'd had a hand in helping his crew earn their solo achievements. Zip had finished with the best time overall, taking the individual award, but he hadn't beat Dev's total time from last year.

Nope, that record still stood and, yeah, Dev had to admit he felt proud of that fact.

There wasn't time for him to find Tanya or his family during the break, but they'd known that when the competition officially started.

Not that he didn't wish he could sneak away—

"Murphy."

He looked up from where he was double-checking the relay team's turnout gear—every member was expected to don a full set including jacket, pants, boots, gloves and helmets—to find the chief standing in front of him.

"Smitty made a mess of his ankle during his last event. He's over at the medical tent getting checked out, but I doubt he'll be able to compete this afternoon."

Dev's heart rose into his throat, even though he knew what the chief was going to say next.

"Osborne is going to be his replacement."

Dev nodded, turning his attention back to his prep work.

"If anyone else goes down, I'm going to need you to step up," the chief continued. "You ready for that?"

He was ready to jump in now, but the order of the alternates wasn't his choice. "Yes, sir."

The afternoon got underway and by the time the final team relay event was being prepped, a race that included all the individual challenges combined, everyone was running on pure adrenaline. While one of the other events was still going on, Dev and Zip got the necessary equipment in order.

"Hey, Murph." Zip tapped him on the arm. "The chief's on his way over."

Dev glanced up and saw him, but kept on working. "Yeah, so?"

"He's got a clipboard in his hand."

Refusing to allow himself to even consider the possibility, Dev tamped down the excitement racing through his veins. "Like I said, probie, yeah, so?"

"So I already signed my form, old man." Zip grinned. "He must be looking for you."

He was.

Another member of the team had been hurt in the last event, called Tug of War, where five members pulled a fire apparatus a set distance using a fire hose as a rope. Destiny had finished a respectable second, but now they were one man down for the relay.

Dev signed the waiver, asked about what position he'd take and then shook the chief's hand before stepping away to make a phone call.

He had to tell Tanya what was happening before she heard his name announced as the teams were called into place.

He found her in the favorites list on his cell phone and hit the button. It took a couple of tries before the call finally went through.

Geez, she was less than a football field away, but it suddenly seemed like she was…

On the other side of the world.

"Hey there." Her sweet voice filled his ear. "You calling to check in?"

Dev pulled in a deep breath, and faced the viewing stands. He knew where his family was sitting, but he couldn't see them. "Having a good time?"

"We all are. This really is an amazing competition."

"It's about to get even more amazing. The team needs me."

There was a long pause, broken only by the crackling noise of static, making him wonder if she was still there. "Tanya?"

"So what are you doing?"

"It's the last event, the team relay. There are five separate sections to the race. Each is timed and in the end the times are compiled to find the winner. I'm going to be doing the Hose Advance Evolution."

"I have no idea what that means."

She could have read about it in the program, after they hung up, but something told Dev she wanted him to explain it to her. "It's the second to last section. I first have to race through a set of orange cones and do my damndest not to knock any over. Then I need to pick up the nozzle end of a charged one-and-three-quarter-inch hose—"

"What does charged mean?"

"An active hose, filled with water," he quickly explained. "I drag it seventy-five feet to a designated mark on the pavement, open the nozzle and hit the target."

More silence on her end.

Dev had no idea what Tanya was thinking. He wanted to see her face-to-face. Her being okay with him doing this meant everything to him, but there wasn't time.

"Well, I guess I'll just say good luck." Her voice wavered a bit, but Dev couldn't tell if that was her or the lousy connection they had. "And, please, be careful."

"I will. I'll look for you afterward in the winner's circle when this is all over, okay?"

The phone went dead and the call abruptly ended. There was no time to call her back.

Dev joined his team as they gathered in the staging area. They watched the other teams that went ahead of them, comparing notes and prepping for their turn.

When the time came, Dev donned his gear, glad he'd been working out with it during the past couple of weeks of training. A cheer went up from the crowd as he took his place and the names of the members of the Destiny team were announced. The bell sounded, and less than three minutes later it was over.

He'd done it.

His time for his section put him in second place, but it was high enough for the Destiny Fire Department to be declared the overall winner.

It took another hour before the awards ceremony, and Dev tried to call Tanya a few times, but finally gave up. After collecting their trophies, the team was surrounded by family, friends and well-wishers, but the only person Dev wanted to see was Tanya.

His brothers and parents found him in the crowd and everyone offered their congratulations, asking him how he'd managed to get on the field. He quickly told the story,

noticing right away that both Tanya and Mac were nowhere to be found.

He finally pulled Liam to the side, demanding to know
where Tanya was, even as a sense of dread filled his chest,
which only grew when his brother told him.

"Why the hell is she going to Chicago today?" he demanded. "Her flight to London doesn't leave until Tuesday night."

"According to Mac, she's leaving tomorrow night instead." Liam crossed his arms over his chest and stared
at him. "I guess because no one was smart enough to ask
her to stay."

Dev realized at that moment how badly he had screwed
up.

He never would've asked Tanya to give up her plans in
London, but he'd never made it clear how much he wanted
her to come home to him after her time there was done.

Or that he planned to join her.

He reached again for his phone, but deep down he knew
this wasn't something he could fix with a simple call.

He needed to get to Chicago. Needed to be at the international terminal when Tanya got there.

No, he needed to be there before she arrived, if he was
going to have any chance at all to make this right.

As Tanya made her way through security at O'Hare
International Airport, there was only one thought on her
mind: how leaving Destiny—leaving Devlin—was the
hardest thing she'd ever done.

She'd taken the coward's way out Sunday afternoon,
but watching Dev in the challenge, watching him win,
had made her realize that if she'd gone to him afterward,
she never would've left him, never would've left Destiny.

She loved him.

She loved his family, the town, the friends she'd made and the private dream she'd been nurturing for a while about returning after her schooling was over to start her own business.

Mac hadn't been happy when she'd insisted on them leaving the competition, but he'd done as she'd asked and drove her back to the cabin to pick up her suitcases, which she'd already packed. She'd loaded them into her car and drove off. She figured she'd be halfway to the airport in Cheyenne before Dev even had a chance to find out she was gone.

Now here she was at another airport even farther from Destiny. After making it past the X-ray scanner at the security checkpoint, she gathered her things, taking special care with her Stetson. She knew it looked a little out of place here in Chicago, but she didn't care.

Her hat was her last link to Dev, and she cherished it.

Setting it back on her head, she slipped on her shoes, put her laptop back in her carry-on and headed for her gate.

The international terminal was a buzz of activity, with people of all nationalities heading in all directions. She truly was excited about London and once she got there, got settled and started her classes, the ache in her chest would lessen a bit.

At least, she hoped so.

Of course, it wouldn't go away entirely. That was impossible, as there was an empty spot there now. She'd left a piece of her heart back in Destiny, and maybe someday...

Refusing to allow herself to make any decisions yet, Tanya reached her gate and searched for a seat along the aisle facing the windows as there was still an hour to go before she boarded.

"Excuse me, miss."

The pretty British accent made Tanya smile. She turned and found an equally pretty airline hostess standing there. But what caught her eye in the crowd at the gate counter was a dark Stetson that stood out among the ball caps and naked heads.

Could it be?

"Are you Miss Reeves?"

Tanya nodded, unable to take her eyes off that hat.

"If you'll come with me, please." The hostess stood to one side and directed Tanya toward the counter. "We need to speak with you about your reservation."

"About my—" The employee's words finally registered. "Is there something wrong?"

"If you'll just follow me."

Tanya did as she was asked, the crowd parting for her as she walked. She tried to keep that familiar Stetson in sight, but after skirting around a busy toddler and his harried mother, she looked up again and the hat was gone.

She pulled in a deep breath and willed the tears to hold off until she could find out what was wrong and get to the privacy of the ladies' room.

Her willpower disappeared, her eyes filling up as she got to the counter and found Dev standing there, a huge bouquet of yellow roses in one hand, his hat in the other.

"Oh, honey, please don't cry."

Too late. The sound of his voice opened the floodgates. She clasped her hands to her mouth, trying to hold back her joy and shock at seeing him right in front of her.

"What are you…" She dropped her hands, pressing them to her chest, and tried again, this time forcing her words to come out louder than a whisper. "How did you get here?"

"Well, thanks to my brothers, your grandfather and a few friends with private planes, I landed in the Windy

City a couple of hours ago." He grinned. "You moving up your departure date took the idea of driving here out of my hands. Besides, I hope to—"

"Wait a minute." She cut him off. "You flew here?"

"Destiny to Cheyenne to Omaha to Chicago."

After Dev had read the official report, they'd talked about the accident in more detail, and he'd mentioned his decision not to ever fly again. As far as Tanya knew, the closest he'd come to being in the air since then was the day he'd climbed inside the family's helicopter and sat there, alone, for hours, trying to come to terms with his demons.

He hadn't made any decisions that day, and she had to respect his process for finding his way back to what he loved most.

To hear he'd taken what sounded like three separate flights to get here...

"Why?" she finally asked. "What are you doing here?"

"Hopefully fixing the biggest mistake of my life."

His words caused her heart to race. Maybe that part of her wasn't so empty, after all. "What mistake is that?"

In three strides Dev was right in front of her, so close she could smell his woodsy cologne and see the bright blue of his eyes. She had to tip her head back to look up at him, loving the certainty in his gaze.

"I love you, Tanya. I've loved you from the moment I saw you and I don't mean just a couple of months ago." His words were low, but a hush had fallen over the crowd, making it easy for everyone to hear him. Especially her. "I fell in love with you one special night ten years ago, but I wasn't ready for you back then. I wasn't ready for the kind of fun and passion and warmth and security you've brought into my life."

"You're ready now?"

"Yes. Spending the past few weeks with you, keeping

my feelings bottled up because I thought that was what was best for you, for me…for us…was my first mistake. The second was letting you leave Destiny without telling you how important you are to me and how much I want you in my life."

He handed her the roses. "Please tell me I'm not too late."

Tanya took the flowers, and when his hand brushed against hers, she grabbed hold of him, loving the relief now shining in his eyes.

Would it still be there after she told him what she had to say?

"I feel the same way about you, but I have to go to London, Dev. I've worked too hard, come too far…in every way, to pass up this chance."

His smile grew as he reached into his suit jacket and pulled out an airline ticket holder. "I know that, honey. I would never ask you to give up your dream. I just want the chance to share it with you. If you want me there."

"But your family…your job…"

"My family is behind me, behind us, one hundred percent, and I can do my job from a flat off Trafalgar Square just as easily as I can from the home office. I'll be traveling back and forth, spending some time in Scotland, too… if you're still looking for a roommate?"

Tanya smiled. "You know, I thought about giving you a week before I called to tell you that you'd better be waiting for me when I came back to Destiny."

That charming grin of his creased his handsome face. "You planned to come back to me?"

The crowd broke into cheers as he pulled her into his arms and kissed her until she was breathless.

"I love you, Devlin Murphy. I love you with all my heart," she whispered against his lips when she able to speak again. "No matter where I am or where I go, I will always be yours. You and I were destined to be together."

And all it had taken was returning to a town whose very name held the promise of forever.

* * * * *

Don't miss Dean Zippenella's story,
the next installment of
USA TODAY *bestselling author*
Christyne Butler's
WELCOME TO DESTINY *series.*
Coming soon from
Harlequin Special Edition.

COMING NEXT MONTH FROM

◆ HARLEQUIN®

SPECIAL EDITION

Available October 22, 2013

#2293 A MAVERICK UNDER THE MISTLETOE
Montana Mavericks: Rust Creek Cowboys
by Brenda Harlen
When Sutter Traub had a falling-out with his family, he took off to Seattle. But now he's back—and so is Paige Dutton, the woman he left behind. Can Sutter and Paige mend their broken hearts together?

#2294 HOW TO MARRY A PRINCESS
The Bravo Royales • by Christine Rimmer
Tycoon Noah Cordell has a thing for princesses—specifically, Alice Bravo-Calabretti. Noah is a man who knows what he wants, but can he finagle his way into this free-spirited beauty's heart?

#2295 THANKSGIVING DADDY
Conard County: The Next Generation • by Rachel Lee
Pilot Edie Clapton saves navy SEAL Seth Hardin's life—and they celebrate with a passionate encounter. Little does Edie know she has a bundle of joy on the way...and possibly the love of a lifetime.

#2296 HOLIDAY BY DESIGN
The Hunt for Cinderella • by Patricia Kay
Fashion designer Joanna Spinelli has nothing in common with straitlaced Marcus Barlow—until they go into business together. Can impetuous Joanna and inflexible Marcus meet in the middle—where passion might ignite?

#2297 THE BABY MADE AT CHRISTMAS
The Cherry Sisters • by Lilian Darcy
Lee Cherry is living the life in Aspen, Colorado. But when she finds herself pregnant from a fling with handsome Mac Wheeler, she panics. Mac follows her home, but little do they know what Love plans for them both....

#2298 THE NANNY'S CHRISTMAS WISH
by Ami Weaver
Maggie Thelan wants to find her long-lost nephew, while Josh Tanner is eager to raise his son in peace. When Maggie signs on, incognito, as Cody's nanny, no one expects sparks to fly, but a true family begins to form....

REQUEST YOUR FREE BOOKS!
2 FREE NOVELS PLUS 2 FREE GIFTS!

⧫ HARLEQUIN®

SPECIAL EDITION
Life, Love & Family

HSE13R

SPECIAL EXCERPT FROM

H HARLEQUIN®

SPECIAL EDITION

*Sutter Traub is a heartbreaker…something Paige Dalton
knows only too well. Which is why she's determined to
stay as far as she can from her ex! But Rust Creek's
prodigal son has come home to help his brother win
an election—and to win back the heart of the woman
he's never been able to forget…*

***

"Sutter?"

He yanked his gaze from her chest. "Yeah?"

She huffed out a breath and drew the lapels closer together.
Despite her apparent indignation, the flush in her cheeks and
the darkening of those chocolate-colored eyes proved that she
was feeling the same awareness that was heating his blood.

"I said there's beer and soda in the fridge, if you want a
drink while you're waiting."

"Sorry, I wasn't paying attention," he admitted. "I was thinking about how incredibly beautiful and desirable you are."

She pushed her sodden bangs away from her face. "I'm a
complete mess."

"Do you remember when we cut through the woods on the
way home from that party at Brooks Smith's house and you
slipped on the log bridge?"

She shuddered at the memory. "It wouldn't have been a big
deal if I'd fallen into water, but the recent drought had reduced

the stream to a trickle, and I ended up covered in muck and leaves."

And when they'd gotten back to the ranch, they'd stripped out of their muddy clothes and washed one another under the warm spray of the shower. Of course, the scrubbing away of dirt had soon turned into something else, and they'd made love until the water turned cold.

"Even then—covered in mud from head to toe—you were beautiful."

"You only said that because you wanted to get me naked."

"Just because I wanted to get you naked doesn't mean it wasn't true. And speaking of naked…"

"I should put some clothes on," Paige said.

"Don't go to any trouble on my account."

***

We hope you enjoyed this sneak peek
from award-winning author Brenda Harlen's
new Harlequin® Special Edition book,
A MAVERICK UNDER THE MISTLETOE,
the next installment in
MONTANA MAVERICKS: RUST CREEK COWBOYS.
Available next month.

HSEEXP1013

SPECIAL EDITION

Life, Love and Family

New! From *New York Times* bestselling author
Rachel Lee

THANKSGIVING DADDY—the next installment in
the *Conard County* miniseries

An Unexpected Family...

Pilot Edie Clapton saves navy SEAL Seth Hardin's
life—and they celebrate with a passionate encounter.
Little does Edie know she has a bundle of joy on the
way...and possibly the love of a lifetime.

Look for THANKSGIVING DADDY next month, from
New York Times bestselling author Rachel Lee.

*Available in November
from Harlequin® Special Edition®,
wherever books are sold.*